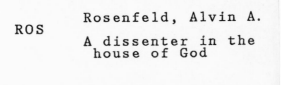

ROS

Rosenfeld, Alvin A.

A dissenter in the
house of God

$15.95

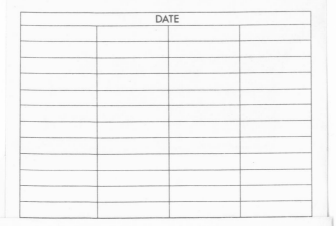

DATE			

© THE BAKER & TAYLOR CO.

A Dissenter in the House of God

Also by Alvin Rosenfeld

The Somatizing Child (with Dr. Elsa Shapiro) non-fiction
Healing the Heart (with Dr. Saul Wasserman) non-fiction

A Dissenter
in the
House of God

ALVIN ROSENFELD

ST. MARTIN'S PRESS · NEW YORK

Design by Judy Dannecker

Library of Congress Cataloging-in-Publication Data

Rosenfeld, Alvin A.
    A dissenter in the house of God / Alvin Rosenfeld.
        p.   cm.
    "A Thomas Dunne book."
    ISBN 0–312–04303–1
    I. Title.
PS3568.08118D57   1990
813′.54—dc20   89–78096

First Edition
10 9 8 7 6 5 4 3 2 1

For my father, Jack.

Acknowledgments

A few people who encouraged me with their words and time deserve special note. My dear friend Peter Winn helped me through more drafts than I care to remember, just as Deb Price helped me in the early stages. My agent, Jane Dystel, was tireless in making sure the book was published by as fine a house as St. Martin's and Thomas Dunne Books. Ruth Cavin, my editor, made numerous suggestions that improved the manuscript. And my beloved wife, Dorothy, kept insisting that this story had to and would be told.

To all of them and to so many other supportive friends I give my sincere and deep thanks.

Chapter One

PRECISELY AT EIGHT A.M. the Friday before Yom Kippur 1955, the Hebrew year 5716, Hyman Schwartz entered the offices of Teitlebaum & Sharfenstein, Accountants, in New York City. He immediately went to his cubicle at the end of a corridor and began working with intense absorption. Moving numbers quickly, methodically lifting them off worksheets and entering them on his adding machine, was Hyman's way of shielding himself from the past.

Many accountants at Teitlebaum & Sharfenstein dressed unfashionably, but Hyman's clothing made a unique statement. He wore a suit that was not simply old; its seams had separated and been resewn innumerable times. Time and wear had polished his pants to a shine. Tape wrapped the plastic bridge on his black-rimmed glasses. And Hyman's overcoat was a veritable patchwork quilt.

That noon, Hyman heard Abromowitz bellow loudly in the corridor. Like everyone else at Teitlebaum & Sharfenstein, he spoke Yiddish. "Come on, Shimshon. It's time for lunch."

To Hyman, Abromowitz looked like a hippopotamus with a black skullcap glued to its head. Abromowitz was not unique in Hyman's affections. He detested all the other accountants as well. For the past few days all they talked about was the upcoming earth-shattering spectacle, the World Series. Dodgers, Yankees. Brooklyn or the Bronx.

Who gave a damn, Hyman thought. He knew that his life would be far simpler if all the other accountants disappeared. Then he could really immerse himself and work in peace.

"Go without me," Hyman heard an unfamiliar voice answer in Yiddish. "I'll catch up."

That unfamiliar voice was close, too close. In fact, when Hyman glanced sideways, he was incredulous. For years he had let everyone know that he wanted no visitors. Yet a man was standing in the doorway to his cubicle.

"Won't you break bread with a newcomer?" the stranger in the doorway asked.

Hyman wished Mr. Teitlebaum had installed doors on the accountants' offices. Then Hyman would never be interrupted.

"Break bread with a *lantzman*," the stranger said, using the Yiddish word for kinsman.

I have no kinsmen, Hyman thought.

"Break bread with *mishpucha*," the man said.

Mishpucha. Family. Don't yell, Hyman told himself. Don't scream. He stared at a worksheet, but the numbers went out of focus. Unable to ignore the Yiddish word, Hyman turned around to see who this provocateur was.

A tall young man was slouched against the metal doorway. Strong, beefy hands emerged from his white shirtsleeves. His shirt's two top buttons were open; the thick hair on his chest cushioned a large, golden star of David. His smile was broad, his eyes were periwinkle blue, the red hair on his head was curly. But the really important fact was that he was an absolute stranger. He's family like my brain is my backside, Hyman thought, and turned back to work.

"Let's eat lunch," the young man persisted. "All the men eat lunch together in the conference room."

Hyman hunched over his adding machine, and punched the black keys as if each of his fingers were a fist smashing the desk in frustration.

"Won't you eat with a kinsman?"

Your words change quicker than a chameleon changes

2

color, and you must have a brain just about as big not to know the difference between kinsman and family.

"At least talk to me."

I'd rather talk to mud. Hyman worried that if this young man pushed him much longer, he might explode. That would ruin everything. The idiot probably has you mixed up with someone else. "I never seen you before, sonny. Get where you're going so I can eat in peace."

"Can't you tell I'm a kinsman? I just came from Budapest."

Although Hyman was sure the man had made a mistake, he turned back and scrutinized him, comparing his features with faces long not seen. Hyman matched the newcomer's voice against others long silent. But no matter how extensively he sifted through his heap of mental ashes, he detected no similarity between this chameleon and people he had once known. "Mr. . . . ?" Hyman said.

"Tisza. But I prefer being called Shimshon."

"Mr. Shimshon . . ."

"Just Shimshon is fine."

"Mr. Just Shimshon. I don't know anyone from Budapest. You got me confused with someone else." Hyman turned back and hurriedly punched ledger entries into his adding machine. "And I eat alone."

"Only a stone stays alone, Mr. Schwartz," Shimshon said, quoting an old Yiddish proverb.

Hyman's calm fractured. This bastard knows my name, this son-of-a-bitch called me *mishpucha* on purpose. To flee before his self-control shattered, Hyman descended into inner space. I hate boys like that. Pushy boys whose teeth shine, whose hands are strong, whose backs are straight. Boys who think they can tease old men because young lions never age. Did you see the way he stands there like no matter where he is, Mama will watch over him, like no matter where he goes everyone will love him as much as she did? I hate boys like that, little bastards who have no idea what life is really like. Maybe it's better that they don't. Maybe we'd all be better off if we never had to learn what life is really like.

Hyman put aside his lunch and started working in earnest.

"I'll be back," Shimshon said. "Tomorrow, the next day, the one after that too. I'm coming back until I understand why you don't recognize a *lantzman* when you see one."

When Shimshon left, Hyman listened to the young man's footsteps recede and felt sunlight again streaming through the unblocked door opening. He cleared his desk so he could finally eat lunch. He sprayed the glass top with Windex and rubbed a smudge until the glass sparkled. No one ever comes back, he thought. Not really.

4

Chapter Two

WHEN THE TAPS of Shimshon's heels had diminished to barely audible clicks and Hyman was certain that Shimshon was not turning back, he stared blankly at the open doorway. Even though he resented Shimshon's uncreased face and optimistic smile, Hyman wanted the young man to return. He would have relished having an opportunity to tell the newcomer one final time what an upstart and bastard he was. After all, even young and stupid boys know not to say they are family to a man who has none.

Hyman finished his lunch and went back to work, but the chronic itch on his arm returned; he scratched himself fiercely through his shirtsleeve. What was a boy Shimshon's age doing coming from Budapest now? Years had passed since anyone new had arrived.

Ten years earlier, in 1945, Sam Teitlebaum had been deeply involved in a project well-to-do American Jews called "the immigrant business." In many east coast and midwestern cities, they had organized successful businessmen into networks that sponsored refugees coming to America from Europe's D.P. camps. They found jobs for these survivors, helped them build lives in the New World, and guaranteed that not one of them would end up on relief. Teitlebaum was very proud to have been involved. "The Talmud says that a man who saves one life has as good as saved the world," he would say years later. "That makes the immigrant business more important than all the money I've ever made." And he meant it. He even had a plaque made that still hung in his office. "I never judge a man who had to be where I did not," it said in ornate Yiddish letters.

Hyman Schwartz did not know that, in the spring of 1955, an uncle of Shimshon's had located Teitlebaum through the old network and put him back, if only briefly, in the immigrant business. Shimshon had waited until his mother died to emigrate. Ultimately, he wanted to set up in Israel as a top accountant. But first he had to learn much more than he knew. Sam agreed to bring him to the States so he could learn at Teitlebaum & Sharfenstein. Sam assigned Abromowitz, one of the better accountants, to teach him.

Shimshon had not been there two days, however, before Sam and other accountants mentioned that the reclusive Hyman Schwartz was by far the best accountant at the firm.

"I want him to teach me," Shimshon told Sam Teitlebaum.

"He won't do it," Sam replied. "Let's say that in addition to being the best, Hyman is different. When I first set eyes on him he was so jumpy I thought they'd used him for medical experiments in Auschwitz. And in 1945, refugees were so desperate for work that every small-town butcher and carpenter not only claimed to have kept books, but swore that he'd kept them for the largest firms in Berlin. So when Hyman said he wasn't an accountant, and insisted that he was telling the truth, I worried that he was crazy. Crazy! Crazy like Einstein. He turned out to be some kind of genius.

"After he had been here for two months, he did more work than most of the men who had been here for years. He claimed he was so good at counting in his head that he didn't need to record his calculations. So he handed in only final ledgers. Well, I told him a thing or two about the real world. I said that in accounting you can be as good as God in your head, but auditors expect records. Hyman's weird, in a funny way absurdly naïve. Without a shred of arrogance, he

6

said, 'I'm not like that. With me you won't need auditors.' He tried to convince me that since he never makes mathematical errors, I'd be wasting my money forcing him to learn to use the adding machine. But if I insisted, he would do it.

"I insisted, and he became excellent entirely on his own. It took me years to realize that he was being absolutely honest about never making errors and was being fussy only because he wanted to save me money. I've never met a man with more exacting standards. If I could see a point to it, I'd ask Hyman to teach you. Unfortunately, he just won't teach anyone."

"Are you sure?" Shimshon said. "He must have his price."

"Not from what I see. He takes at most a quarter of what he makes from me and hands back the rest. He lives at some run-down hotel and eats his meals at the Automat. When Hyman had been here for a year, the salary that he left with me had become a substantial sum. I asked him what to do with it. He squinted at me like I was sad or stupid, maybe both. 'Keep it. Spend it. Put it someplace good,' he said. 'What do I need it for?' So I invest it. He's never once asked whether he's made or lost money. Dollars mean nothing to that man."

"And people?"

"Less." Sam shook his head. "I've invited Hyman to my house fifty times, but he's never accepted. Years ago, the men tried to include him in their circle, but after the twentieth rebuff they stopped asking. Since Faye started working for me last year, she asked him to join her for coffee a number of times, I guess out of pity, and probably because it was not long after her husband died. But Hyman always says he's too busy."

Shimshon looked perplexed.

"Settle for Abromowitz," Sam said.

"I want to try Hyman."

"Aren't you stubborn." Sam smiled. "And persistent. I like that. So go ask him today, tomorrow, any day after. You'll find him in his cubicle at the end of the corridor, under the exit sign, wearing the same clothes I bought him the day he came here."

"Why don't you ask him to buy new ones?"

"I don't know him well enough."

"After ten years?"

"Of everyone in this office, I'm probably the one Hyman is closest to. And he acts like I carry the plague." Sam sighed and looked Shimshon up and down. "If you are really determined to have the best teach you, Hyman has to be your first choice. Go try him. You'd learn more from that man in a month than you'd learn from the rest of this office in a year. When he first came here, Hyman wouldn't teach. But you might just be persistent enough to get him to reconsider."

"Wouldn't he be more likely to reconsider if you asked?"

"I'm more likely to get God to tap-dance. Hyman may appreciate me. But he looks at me like he's saying, 'Do this American and I have anything in common?' You're European, Shimshon. Talk to him. If you get Hyman Schwartz to teach you, you'll learn how the best accountant in this firm thinks." Sam paused for a moment. "Now something else, Shimshon. I told my wife about you. She wants you to join us for Yom Kippur."

"You don't even know me, Mr. Teitlebaum."

"The name is Sam. You're a Jewish man with no place to be for Kol Nidre Sunday night and for Yom Kippur Monday. And I'm a Jewish man with a big house. That's knowing you well enough. I even have an extra seat at synagogue. Mildred's father, old faithful himself, changed his mind and decided to go to the Pine View Hotel for the High Holy Days."

"But I don't fast."

"And we don't lock the refrigerator. So around three this Sunday, take the BMT Brighton Line train to the Avenue J stop." Sam wrote on a piece of paper, and handed it to Shimshon. "That's my home number. Call me when you're at Avenue J and I'll pick you up at the station. And Tuesday morning, I'll bring you back to the office so Mr. Ambitious can begin working bright and early."

Chapter Three

AS HYMAN WENT BACK to his computations after Shimshon's visit, a tear fell on the worksheet in front of him. Don't do that, he told himself. You spent too long crying and fainting. Now's the season for keeping ledgers perfectly straight. Here: 345 times 999. Come on, Hyman Schwartz. You know exactly how much that is.

It would not work. Time had folded on itself. Then was now, now was then. Nineteen thirty-nine had returned. Hyman's little boy was running toward him on their Warsaw street, arms outstretched, yelling "Papa, Papa. You're home." Hyman smashed the desk and wished he could do the same to the lousy lying Shimshon who had brought the memories back.

Shimshon was almost the right age to be David, just a few years older. If David were alive . . . If. If my aunt had wheels she would be a truck. The numbered ones had stopped trickling in seven or eight years earlier. It's 1955 now, Hyman thought. Shimshon was a boy from after the war.

Enter numbers meticulously or you'll begin making mistakes like the Great Monster himself, Hyman told himself. Pay attention to what needs attention: make sure every credit and debit match. Be careful. Be so meticulous that no Fancy-Dan auditor can ever say you've cheated. Concentrate.

Hyman could not. David and Rachel would not leave his thoughts. When the office closed, he went to the Automat for dinner. But that night and all the next day, he kept remembering what he had spent years trying to forget.

Sunday was Yom Kippur Eve. In the late afternoon, Hyman headed toward Central Park. A warm sun soothed lovers and families strolling the footpaths. Blooming roses swayed over trellis tops; red petals rustled in the breeze.

Hyman did not appreciate the soothing weather; seasons long past enshrouded him. The dirt paths near Hecksher Playground reminded him of a day in August 1939 when David and he were walking in Warsaw's Praga Park and approached a man giving children pony rides. Hyman put his three-and-a-half-year-old son astride the piebald pony. David insisted on keeping a twig he had picked up.

Hyman had retrieved a photograph from that day. Oh yes. He had the pictures, even though he dared not look at them. He remembered David smiling, holding that stick aloft, saying, "And that's my sword, Papa, King David's sword."

Now Hyman wandered the park aimlessly, as if by heading down a footpath or past a meadow he could transform himself into a zombie, escaping a past that had evaporated and left only pain. That transformation had become as natural to Hyman as the annual transfiguration from green to gold was to leaves in Central Park. But this weekend was different. Someone new had arrived from Europe.

Hyman recalled the day when he had staggered into Warsaw certain that David and Rachel would also return. He had made his way to their apartment. But nothing remained. Nothing but two cold stairs and two smashed columns standing amid a heap of rubble. At that moment, he had decided to perfect his skill at counting numbers in his head. For years he had practiced and nurtured the method. Numbers were his refuge, his last defense against the complete loss of reason. How much is 222 times 999? It's 221,778 of course. But stop asking simple questions. Move to hard computations. Move. Walk. Get away.

10

He walked faster. His clothes felt rough, itching him mercilessly and setting his skin on fire. He reached under his shirtsleeves and scratched; his fingernails raised long welts on his forearms. Control yourself or you'll go entirely mad, he commanded himself. Control yourself, Hyman Schwartz, or they'll put you away too. He walked and calculated, checking his watch repeatedly, hoping the hands would turn more quickly and that the interminable work-free days would end. At five forty-five, he left the park's Eighty-first Street exit and went south. Head down, he stared at cracks in the sidewalk. On Seventy-second Street, he looked left to check the traffic before crossing. As he looked right, up the street canyon before him, toward Riverside Drive, Hyman saw that the setting sun had painted the sky red and was bathing the uptown buildings in rosy light. Down Seventy-second Street, on the northern side, Hyman noticed a woman his age hurrying up the steps to a large building. He walked over and saw CONGREGATION BETH EL chiseled into a light-reddened lintel over the wide doorway.

He stood there struck and paralyzed. He had not been in a synagogue for over ten years. You've got no reason to go in, he told himself. But then he thought, They would want me to.

Dead people don't want anything, he answered back. "Do it!" he heard himself say. As if in a trance, he found himself ascending the stairs. He passed between the polished marble columns and walked through the open doors. Why does this have to be the place, he wondered, a house He had filled with wails, lamentations and pleas?

Hyman looked through the main prayer hall's open door and saw a sea of three-piece suits and heard the rustle of women's dresses. He watched the rabbi sliding aside the holy ark's doors. Congregants were coming to attention as they faced the Torahs in the ark. On the polished oak floor an army of sneakers squeaked. No observant congregant in an Orthodox synagogue would wear leather shoes today; the support they provided was forbidden on the Day of Atonement.

11

At the entrance, a beadle handed a prayer book to each congregant. Hyman looked down at his old, cracked wing-tips, waved the beadle off and entered empty-handed. Walking past the center aisle to a space behind the last bench, he listened to the cantor intoning the mournful Kol Nidre prayer. That beautiful melding of sorrow with hope actually had made Hyman weep once upon a time when he was young and uninformed. The prayer pleaded with the Lord to forgive vows, obligations and sins. Hyman closed his ears and steeled his heart.

The two huge walls on the synagogue's sides had six stained-glass windows, each with a different animal or symbol that commemorated an ancient tribe of Israel. Synagogues in Rava and Belz, where Hyman had grown up, had been plain, their white plaster walls unadorned. There, stained-glass windows were no more Jewish than a church.

Beth El's congregants responded to the cantor's song. "Forgive all my sins," they prayed to God. "Forgive my vows." Hyman remained silent. My papa took me to synagogue on Yom Kippur, he remembered. I begged God to make my sins light and to blow them away like feathers. I was so young then. I actually believed that God kept meticulous books and scrutinized His creations on Yom Kippur to decide who deserved to live, who to die.

Light from the setting sun transformed the stained-glass windows on the left into flowing curtains of rubies, sapphires, emeralds and topazes. Spots of color showered the synagogue's interior. Hyman watched the congregants pray. To him, they looked like frogs on colored lily pads, erect amphibians who pounded their breastbones as their gaping mouths enumerated transgressions. "Forgive my sins. Forgive my vows. Forgive the days and weeks and months I've strayed from Your righteous path. I have lied. I have sinned. I have stolen. I have offended You," all the congregants, even the innocents, said in unison. The prayer chilled Hyman's bones and made him shiver. Only a species of idiot would ask for His forgiveness.

Reflexively, Hyman began practicing calculations. But he stopped for a moment when he recognized a face beside the aisle near the synagogue's front. Jack Rossberg, a client of the firm, whispered to his young boy. The boy looked puzzled. Mr. Rossberg smiled, whispered in his ear, and pointed in the siddur to the page the cantor was singing from. The boy smiled back. Hyman watched Rossberg lift his arm and drape the boy in his prayer shawl as if it were an eagle's wing promising protection.

An eagle. Protection. The boy's smile and Mr. Rossberg's embrace made Hyman turn back to the opened ark immediately. He concentrated harder on calculations, moving numbers more quickly through his mind.

The time for Kaddish, the prayer for the dead, approached. Shaken out of his numerological trance, Hyman felt the sacred time upon him, entering him. A force inside rumbled; shrieks pressed toward his lips. About to lose his self-control, he turned toward the door to leave, but strength had ebbed from his legs. He tried to calculate, to calm himself with numbers, but could not. Steadying himself on the beveled top of the bench in front of him, Hyman edged himself sideways.

He stopped just before the center aisle beside a tall, somber man. He stared directly down the maroon runner, past the pew where Rossberg and his son sat, past the elevated *bimah* from which the cantor sang, up the stairs to the platform where the rabbi prayed. The Torahs stood erect and proud in the ark's heart, with silver crowns on their heads and embroidered velvet jackets covering their parchment scrolls.

The rabbi and the congregation stood, looked inward in sorrow, and began reciting the rhythmic beat of the Kaddish. *"Yisgadal veyiskadash schmei rabba."* ("Until the world's end, let Thy Glory and Thy Kingdom reign.")

Now Hyman realized why he had entered: he had been anticipating this confrontation for years. Too much had happened for him to pray to God. Maybe the tall man next to him could. Maybe Jack Rossberg could. Maybe everyone else in the synagogue could pray to the Lord Almighty, King of the Universe. But Hyman's experience was too extensive to simply pray as if the Lord reigned with balanced books. He had come to ask an important question. Hyman looked at the Torahs. "Did you see them lead David and Rachel away?" he said out loud.

The tall man beside Hyman nudged him. "Shh."

Hyman stopped speaking, but his private interrogation continued. I have to ask. When they pray to the King of the Universe, whom exactly do they pray to? Because if You were in charge, anyone with a brain would leave right now and burn this place to the ground.

Recollections flooded back. Rage threatened Hyman's control of his mind.

If You weren't present, let me tell You what I saw and what others told me happened. Because when You're brought to trial, I don't want You asking oh, so innocently, why no one ever told You. Listen, King of the Universe. If You think that only converts, gamblers, and whores were in the cattle cars, think again. *Everyone* was there. Your servants. Your enemies. Very religious with one side of their beards cut off. Ordinary people like Yankel Jaffe, the tailor, and Blimah Silverstein, the shoemaker's wife.

Later I heard that, not far from the railway dock, all the ones who went right had to take off their clothes. Even shtetl Hasidim, men who were so strict they wouldn't kiss their own daughters, had to stand naked with women. They covered their penis and testicles with their hands and looked away. Yeshiva students begged their teachers, "Isn't it time for the Messiah to come?" Rabbis stared at the ground because they didn't know what to answer. "What mortal can read God's clock?" Don't think there weren't rabbis who had as many questions as I do. In the cattle car I heard more than one say he didn't know where God went. But even the doubters prayed Shema to You in the cars and on the line. "Hear O Israel. The Lord is our God. The Lord is One." Day or night, winter or summer, Jews on their way to the gas promised that until time ends they would have only one God. You.

The Kaddish proceeded in its traditional slow rhythmic cadences. "Thy name is holy and blessed," rolled off five hundred lips. But Hyman's lips were silent. The memories flooded on, red and vivid. His legs shook; his mind shuddered.

Not everyone was religious when they came. Some people got religious right there on the railway dock. Maybe they figured that if they became like Kohanim of old and pronounced "Jehovah" just right, they might finally see God's mercy.

Hyman looked up at the pale blue dome in the center of the ceiling and was amazed. For years he had managed not to visualize anything. And now somehow Shimshon's intrusion had triggered the visions again.

On the dome Hyman saw the railway dock, and standing on it were Gittel and Yankelah, a mother and son who had been squeezed together beside him in the cattle car. They sent me to the left. But I watched her walk away with the line of people who went to the right. Six-year-old Yankelah held one arm around his mother's leg, and sucked his other fist. Sucking became biting so quickly that Gittel didn't see that her son's teeth had broken his skin until blood dripped down his chin. Before they were ten yards away, a Gestapo man butted his rifle into Gittel's back screaming, "Move, you Jewish bitch. Move." But Gittel lifted Yankelah to her chest before she started to move. She whispered patiently in her son's ear and took his hand out of his mouth.

We all say the King of the Universe is perfect. But that one simple woman behaved the way I never saw the great King act. Where in the middle of that madness she found the strength must be a secret women keep. She walked, carrying her boy, and sang to him: "Tumbala, tumbala, tumbalala. Tumbala, oy tumbalala." If the song had had real words, even Gittel couldn't have sung it. It made no difference.

Within ten minutes only the twenty of us in my line were left. "Move quick. Move quicker," they said to starving people. "Don't you know? Toast and marmalade are waiting? Move quick." Move quicker. Be fooled sooner. Turn to ashes now so I can smell your guts burned in this afternoon's air. "Move quick. Move now. Move you Jewish bitch." That Gestapo bastard pushed Gittel. I was standing in the line headed the other way. I saw it. If I really was a man I would have killed him.

The man praying beside Hyman approached the end of his Kaddish. "He who makes peace in His heavens . . ."

The *Sonderkommando* were Jews who took bodies from the chambers and pulled gold from the teeth. One I spoke to told me that in every chamber, at least one mother had wrapped herself around her child. I'm sure Gittel did that. She loved her boy so much she wouldn't let him die alone. When she wrapped herself around him, was she trying to force Yankelah back inside the way he was before he was born? Or did she think that if she wrapped herself entirely around him, she could keep the poison air away? Shouldn't a God who reigns over heaven and earth have some idea how people feel, how He makes them suffer?

"He who makes peace in His heavens shall make Peace on this Earth, descend, upon us and upon all the nation of Israel, and say ye Amen." Kaddish had ended. The synagogue was silent.

Hyman pointed a shaking finger at the dome and screamed. "He killed them."

People all over the synagogue turned back and stared at Hyman. Jack Rossberg's son tugged nervously at his father's prayer shawl and whispered in his ear. The rabbi rushed to the lectern, grasped its sides, and stared at Hyman as if rabbinical authority alone would silence him. Next to him the tall man implored. "Please, mister. I buried my Sadie only three weeks ago. Please let Him hear her name."

"Your Sadie?" Hyman pulled away. "Ask the bastard who stabbed you to sew you back together."

"Shh . . . ," the man said.

"Silence, please," the rabbi said.

Stunned congregants whispered to one another; two men rushed toward the synagogue's rear, their prayer shawls streaming behind them.

Hyman looked at the dome as if he could see the stars beyond. "You killed them. You did it."

All eyes in Beth El were on Hyman when the two men reached him. "Please, let's go outside to talk," one of them said.

"It was You!" Hyman screamed. His face was red and puffy; tears streamed down his cheeks.

The men lifted Hyman by his arms and carried him, struggling and screaming, toward the door. When Hyman stopped to catch his breath, the rabbi spoke. "Please, my dear friend. Please show respect for the Kaddish."

"Sure!" Hyman screamed. "Respect the biggest murderer of them all."

"Please, sir," the rabbi said, his face blood-red.

Hyman tried to pull free, but the men held his arms tightly and carried Hyman, kicking and screaming, out to the synagogue's front steps. He struggled and cursed them, but they still held tight. Finally, he comprehended what one of them was saying: "Just stop screaming and we'll let you go." Hyman clenched his teeth and stifled his voice. When the men let go of his arm, he crumpled to the ground. One man knelt and put his hand on Hyman's trembling shoulder. "Can I help you?"

"Help me?" Hyman had been struggling to contain himself. Now he laughed maniacally. "Do you really want to help somebody who needs it? Help God!"

Hyman staggered over to a tall gray pillar. Clutching its glassy surface, he struggled to regain control. His legs buckled and his palms squeaked on the surface; he slid to his knees sobbing. But along with his agony, he felt proud of himself. He felt alive. Finally, he had said it all. He actually had stood straight up in synagogue, pointed at the dome, and publicly accused the Schwartz family's murderer to His face.

He heard someone else coming out. "I know what you've been through Mr. Schwartz," a man said.

Hyman looked to the side and saw Jack Rossberg crouching beside him. He felt Rossberg's hand on his shoulder.

"Spend tonight with my family."

And spend all night staring at your son? Hyman pushed himself up, looked at Rossberg as if he were crazy, and rushed away.

Chapter Four

SCENES FROM THE CAMPS pursued him. His pride dissipated in the evening chill. The righteousness he had felt wavered before the doubts and accusations that hounded his mind. Can a mortal teach the Lord honesty? Didn't Papa say that any man who blasphemes the Lord commits one of the ten gravest sins? By Sixty-seventh Street, Hyman had lost his courage. By Sixty-fifth he had become a stooped, terrified man again. God's glowering eyes filled the sky, His raging voice boomed. "Hyman Schwartz. Fleck of dirt on My perfect earth. You violated My house, you desecrated My scrolls."

"You killed my family," Hyman countered. But his voice sounded hollow; courage and self-righteousness seeped away like water through sand.

"You violated My sanctuary and cursed My name."

At Sixty-second Street an ambulance screamed down Central Park West. Hyman was afraid. Had he given God more reason to punish him? Would God place this outburst in the debit column so He could justify sending back *Achtung!*'s and cattle cars to Buna?

Hyman went right past the Excelsior Hotel, where he lived. Discomposed, he rushed downtown. At the corner of Forty-fifth Street, the Camel man on the billboard across Broadway smoked his perpetual cigarette. His hair was straight, his face rugged, his nose classic, his cigarette a

19

Camel. From the center of his confident lips, smoke rings puffed out. Suddenly incandescent-white in the spotlights, the rings rippled, misted, and dissipated into the black night. Hyman inhaled fearfully, expecting Buna's stench. But the air smelled like burnt coffee grounds; no more, no less.

Stay in the light, he told himself. Stay away from manholes, shadows, and black alleys. There's danger in every corner of this damned world. Stay in the light.

He entered a square of soft, yellow light under the Shubert theater's marquee just as a smiling crowd made its way out of *South Pacific*. Brushed by men in vicuña coats, jostled by women whose diamonds flashed rainbows into the theater night, Hyman was alone. Laughing theatergoers who celebrated the here and now were animated forms, peacocks and orangutans who lived in a mirage with no idea of what human life was really like.

Since the day Hyman had disembarked at the Thirty-second Street wharf, time had been frozen. He knew he was not one of them. He had matured in Warsaw, glorious home to Stare Miasto, the Bristol Hotel, cafés and broad, carriage-filled esplanades. On good days, he vaguely remembered the old world, a Warsaw whose buildings stood proud, tall, and elegant, a Warsaw where Rachel's kisses soothed him, where meals were rich and home was comfortable.

He still believed that Rachel could not be just a Kaddish to be said. Her soft hands would soothe him again, her delicious lips would kiss him again. That was what he had screamed. No to the powder blue dome. No to the clock's hands. No to the future. No to ever saying Kaddish for Rachel. She will be my wife until time ends.

A soft young woman accidentally bumped into Hyman. She apologized. Turning back, she looped her arm inside her boyfriend's and snuggled into his shoulder.

Hyman watched the boyfriend kiss her cheek and saw her draw him closer in reply. I won't ever forgive God. I won't ever feel for another woman, he thought, rushing away from the theater.

For the next eight hours Hyman wandered New York's streets. He saw the last diners speed away in cabs, and watched the haggard owners of French restaurants on Fifty-sixth Street pull down the shades, turn off the lights and lock up at two in the morning. He saw streetwalkers on Forty-first Street and Tenth Avenue plying their trade until all drunken sailors, salesmen, and conventioneers had stumbled back to their rooms. What kind of world is this? he thought as he watched one call girl, a pink feather boa around her neck, climb out of a limousine on Fifty-second Street. She sashayed right past Hyman as if he did not exist.

He wandered through that black time around four A.M. Monday morning when everyone sleeps and even New York City's streets doze for an hour. Just before five, Hyman passed a derelict sifting through a trash can's newspapers, crumpled paper bags, candy wrappers and empty bottles. When the man saw Hyman staring at him, he stood up straight and stared back. "What are ya starin' at, bub?" the man said. "You don't look so different from me."

Hyman turned away quickly.

"Hey, buster. I had a job once too." The derelict held out his hand. "How about helpin' a buddy. I need a quarter. That's what I'm lookin' for. Ya lookin' for something too, mister?"

"I don't know myself." Hyman looked back at the derelict. Shaking his head, he reached in his pocket and handed over a crisp dollar bill. Before the incredulous man could respond, Hyman left.

The horizon turned apricot-colored at five forty-five. By six, dawn was slipping thin yellow fingers of light through interstices between the buildings. The light turned a spray truck rumbling down Forty-eighth Street into gold and ignited the cellophane wrappers and cigarette butts its water showered toward the curb. It set the slaked streets ablaze.

Hyman walked close to the buildings to avoid the spray of a sanitation truck. A car's tires hissed over the shiny damp blacktop. A truck delivering bundled morning papers swished past moments later. The air filled with the sweet fragrance of water evaporating and of fresh coffee brewing in the shops. Hyman knew that he had to get back to his room before people crowded the streets. He had to be alone, conjuring up the numbers that made pain diminish and memories disappear.

At six fifteen, he entered the Excelsior Hotel's lobby and tiptoed up the staircase. He was tired, contrite and shivering. Standing beside his bed, Hyman dropped his clothes, piece by piece, to the floor—his overcoat, his old suit jacket, the worn slacks, pilled tie, frayed white shirt and underwear, all in a crumpled pile. He staggered to his closet stark naked and pulled down an old woolen blanket. Curling up on the floor just beyond the carpet's edge, he wrapped the blanket around himself.

He tried to eat several times in the next eighteen hours lest he create the mistaken impression, even to himself, that he was observing God's mandated fast. But he could not. Nauseated, he shivered uncontrollably. To his eyes, the ceiling, the walls, and the doors had become screens on which scenes from the camps were projected. Trains, lines, ashes. There was Gittel comforting Yankelah on the ceiling. Hyman turned toward the door, but there she was wrapped around her son, trying to save him from the gas. He shut his eyes, but the visions would not disappear. Nor would her song. He heard Gittel's "Tumbala" playing in his mind. Hyman stuck a finger in each ear, but her soft melody played on. Did Rachel sing to David when she realized where they were going? he wondered.

Long after the first three stars twinkled in the evening sky, the official sign that Yom Kippur had ended, Gittel still enfolded Yankelah in every corner of Hyman's room. His bladder was ready to burst, but he had neither the strength nor the motivation to walk to the toilet down the hall. He staggered to the sink against the wall and, for the first time since coming to New York, Hyman urinated in it. Watching the yellow rivulet flow toward the drain, he was horrified.

He remembered the *Musselmen* he had seen in Buna, the walking dead who had given up and were ready to die. Only they would drink piss water. Disgusted, Hyman curled back up on the floor. What's happening to me? What did that Shimshon do to me? What am I becoming? Why did I talk to God? So He can also steal my pride?

All night long, Hyman lay on those planks shivering. He tried to conjure up mathematical formulas that would make everything but the wondrous world of Pythagoras, Boole, Gödel, and numbers disappear.

At six on Tuesday, he took out fresh underwear, picked his clothes up off the floor, and dressed for work. A night spent counting numbers in his head finally had turned off the visions and silenced the melody. Just count numbers, Hyman told himself. Count numbers so no one can guess what you did. Be especially careful that Mr. Teitlebaum doesn't see you today. Don't ever let the boss know how bad off you can get. And stay away from Shimshon. That bastard brings out the worst in you.

As usual, Hyman walked to Horn & Hardart's Automat. He forced himself to finish a bowl of hot oatmeal and a cup of black coffee. Eat so you don't faint, he told himself. Eat so you don't lose your job. Without it you'll go completely mad and fly into a million pieces. Hold yourself together. Eat. You know how quickly things can disappear. Eat. A man who once ate vulture bones can keep down cereal. Eat or you'll ruin everything.

Chapter Five

HYMAN WAS STANDING at the door precisely when Faye
Sondheimer, Sam Teitlebaum's secretary, unlocked it at
eight. He hurried to his cubicle. Relieved to immerse himself in habit, he opened a worksheet and took a box of
Ticonderoga number-two pencils out of his top drawer.
(Hyman never used number-one pencils—their lead was
too soft, his numbers would smudge.) He followed the
identical pattern every day, doing each worksheet on two
separate mornings, checking it on two afternoons. On the
first morning of each two-day sequence, he checked the
arithmetic on every invoice. If it was correct, he wrote the
amount credited or debited in the appropriate worksheet
column. After entering all figures, he computed the balance
on his adding machine, wrote the totals at the worksheet's
bottom and stapled the narrow adding machine record to
its back. Then he checked his calculations in the way he
trusted most, in his head. If the two results matched, Hyman started the next worksheet.

Late each morning, Hyman did a third check of worksheets begun the morning before. After a brief lunch, he
rechecked each entry to make sure he had transcribed the
invoices accurately. He recalculated every sheet in his head
and on his adding machine one final time late on the second
afternoon. If the calculations matched (they always did), he

took out a fountain pen, hesitated because he felt reverence for steps that were irrevocable, and carefully transcribed the results into the appropriate ledger book.

Hyman was so obsessional that seeing him work should have been about as interesting as watching a slug. Actually it was thrilling. He became so thoroughly absorbed in work that his fingers played like a concert pianist's. Invoices, credits, debits and balances flowed through his fingers in graceful rhythms. And he was more than just fast and rhythmic; he was meticulous, which allowed him to complete twice the number of worksheets than other men who worked well. His work never needed painstaking review to unearth simple errors. To Hyman, a mathematical error was a tragedy. So he dedicated himself to avoiding them entirely.

And he always wanted to be busy. "Give me more work," he told Sam whenever his workload slackened. "Give me more work."

Once he had immersed himself in the adding machine's rhythm, Yom Kippur night disappeared. Only depreciation schedules, running balances, and the elegant format of accounting statements remained. Today nothing broke Hyman's concentration. Just after noon he stopped for a brief lunch. Although he wished he could avoid that interruption too, years had taught him that his body needed fuel to keep working swiftly. After all, even a horse needs oats.

Hyman got out the food he had bought at Horn & Hardart's, and had just begun to sip his water when a shadow came between him and the noontime sun.

"Won't you join a kinsman for lunch?" Shimshon said.

Hyman sipped his water.

"I told you I would be back," Shimshon went on. "What are you doing, giving me the silent treatment?"

If your chameleon brain is big enough to figure that out, it ought to be smart enough to get you out of here. Hyman bit into his chicken sandwich.

"So when will we eat together?" When Hyman continued to ignore him, Shimshon stepped into the cubicle.

"Get out!" Hyman snapped.

Shimshon stepped back and slouched against the door-frame.

Hyman wanted to be back at worksheets and ledgers. But he did not want to give any hint of what he had done Kol Nidre night. So he decided to be civil to Shimshon. "I've got important work to do, Mr. Just Shimshon, and you're making it harder."

"We still haven't eaten lunch together."

"And we never will! Why not be a good boy and go away." Although Hyman felt his anger well up, he actually was hungry; he ate more of his sandwich.

Shimshon asked whether they could eat together Wednesday.

Hyman threw away the rest of the sandwich, polished his desktop, opened a black ledger book on his lap and began going through it. Then he heard Shimshon's footsteps receding down the hallway.

On Thursday, Hyman checked his watch a dozen times between eleven thirty and twelve. Just before noon on Friday, he heard Himmelstein talking loudly to Abromowitz as they walked down the corridor toward the conference room. "We all knew they were bums. So why did I get my hopes up? They dropped two in a row. Those Bums have no chance of winning and never did."

"Don't pay off your bets yet," Abromowitz said. "You don't count out Snider, Furillo, Campanella, Newcombe, Hodges, Robinson, Erskine and Reese."

"I'm telling you. With Alston starting a pitcher like Podres today, you can say bye-bye to this year. Podres won nine and lost ten this year. The Dodgers never win the big one. It's always the same. Nineteen forty-one, forty-seven, forty-nine, fifty-two, fifty-three and now fifty-five. You can sneak out to listen to the game today, Abromowitz. I'd get more pleasure going to the dentist."

They're just imbeciles to think some sport is important in life, Hyman thought.

Right at noon Shimshon arrived. Hyman watched him settle his shoulder on the doorframe. When he was certain he had Shimshon's attention, he pulled up his left shirtsleeve and scrutinized Shimshon's face, anticipating the squint or wince that would confirm that this boy had finally seen and comprehended. But Shimshon never gave any indication that he noticed the five blue numbers seared into Hyman's forearm.

As the days went by, Shimshon's approach had become more subtle. Since Hyman had bristled at familiarity, he addressed Hyman as Mr. Schwartz and stopped provoking him by calling him family. On Friday, when Hyman reacted less hostilely, Shimshon lingered a few minutes longer. Although what they developed over those first days was not a relationship, it was a protocol. Shimshon jabbered, and Hyman parried with single words and short phrases. At twelve fifteen, Shimshon always suggested that he wanted to eat lunch with his colleague, at which point Hyman swiveled back to his adding machine and started entering numbers.

"I'll be back," Shimshon said. When Hyman continued working, Shimshon reiterated his promise and left.

When Shimshon told Sam about these encounters, Sam was surprised that Hyman had spoken at all. He told Shimshon that, from the sound of it, the young man was getting somewhere. So he encouraged Shimshon to proceed.

And Hyman was affected. By the time Shimshon had returned for the fourth consecutive workday, Hyman found himself wondering how old the bastard—in Yiddish, the *mamzer*—from after the war really was. He guessed that Shimshon was not all that much older than David would have been. Hyman yearned for David and hungered for Rachel. Since he had screamed at the Lord, Hyman was able to remember the perfume Rachel had worn. He could smell it now; Buna's chimneys no longer camouflaged its fragrance.

But he knew that sentimentality threatened equanimity. To yearn for what could never be, to remember softness that had vanished forever, was the one sure route to madness.

Think like a rational being, he ordered himself. Work on the Ziegel Underwear books. They depreciated sewing machines at higher-than-normal third-year levels. Check the tables. Don't waste valuable time. Get working or you'll make a mistake that the boss will get rid of you for. And what will you have then to hold back the memories?

But every day, just after the *mamzer* left, Hyman sat immobile for a moment, his eyes riveted on his tattoo. More than anything else, those five blue numbers reminded him of who he was, of where he had been, and of what he had lost.

Chapter Six

THE FEAST OF TABERNACLES' first days were Saturday and Sunday. Hyman found himself, against his will, thinking about Shimshon. Where had he come from? Who does he have? He's young enough to be my son. Where is David now? Hyman knew that he should not have asked that last question. Wondering made him so edgy that he raised long red welts on the back of his hand with his fingernails. Since Shimshon's noontime visits were more than a broken heart could bear, Hyman decided that the next time that *mamzer* bothered him, he would chase the little bastard away.

When Shimshon slouched against the doorjamb the next Monday and repeated his standard invitation, Hyman told him that he had suffered enough disruption to his routine and wished to be left alone in the future.

"Why not teach me accounting?" Shimshon said. "Someone must have taught you."

"I taught myself. If you want to learn accounting, ask an educated specialist to teach you."

"But everyone says that you're the best."

"The best?" Hyman faced Shimshon. "I do my job. But you should learn accounting from a man who studied it."

"Sam studied accounting and he said that the best man to learn from is you. He said you do the work of two men and three horses. He also warned me that even though you work like a horse, you behave like a mule."

Hyman was amused. "That makes us a fine pair. One mule, one jackass."

"Mule or not, Sam said you should teach me."

"That I don't believe," Hyman answered, running his finger down a worksheet.

"Ask him whether he said that you're the best."

"Mr. Teitlebaum says lots of things. And as you can see, Mr. Just Shimshon, you're interrupting my work." Hyman immersed himself in the adding machine's rhythm until Shimshon's voice was simply a distant murmuring.

Shimshon looked annoyed. "Also ask Sam why he said you and I were almost like family."

Hyman whipped around. "Mr. Teitlebaum never said that."

"Ask him," Shimshon said. He shot a challenging smile at Hyman. "See you tomorrow," he said and strutted off.

I suffered enough in this life, Hyman thought. Does God have to send new monsters to cut my guts? Family. In Hyman's mind's eye, the years fled in disarray and 1943 returned. Torahs shriveled as they burned. On the ghetto streets, loudspeakers on truck roofs boomed commands. "*Achtung!* Assemble now. *Achtung!*" Hyman had heard those trucks so many times, he could not believe he had missed the one that counted.

He remembered going to an office in the ghetto. The Nazis had ordered fathers to pay an enormous sum of money to buy tickets so their wives and children could be resettled in the east. How stupid I was, Hyman thought, recalling how he had paid and where his beloved had actually been sent.

But the Gestapo had not waited for the resettlement date. Why did he have to be out hunting for essentials when the Nazis made their surprise roundup? David had pleaded with him not to go out that day. If only he had been at home, if only he could have gone with them.

In his mind, Hyman recounted the events as a neighbor

from across the street had described them. He had replayed the scene so many times in his mind, he no longer knew whether he was recalling the neighbor's account or how he had adapted it. David and Rachel were herded into a crowd. David's floppy, flat-topped cap and woolen coat were too small for his growing body. His trusting brown eyes looked up, hoping that his papa would be back at the window to move with the family. David had waved one last good-bye. "Hands up, hands up," sound trucks ordered. In a winter breeze that blew her coat open, Rachel had shown David how to obey rifles. Raising her defeated hands over her head, she marched off near the head of a crowd with David beside her.

Trees became stumps, people became ashes. Gittel tried to engulf Yankelah. And the earth vomited bones and flesh that seduced vultures into the sky. Family. Does that *mamzer* realize he's dancing on ashes?

Although he was infuriated, Hyman knew he had to be careful. If Mr. Teitlebaum had recommended that he teach the *mamzer*, it was the boss's first request in years. But more than a job or a boss's desires influenced Hyman. When he stared at Shimshon's strong hands, amazed by the confident way they emerged from inside his sleeves, he recalled hoping that his David would grow up to be big and strong.

Stop, Hyman thought. I have important things to do, like finishing a complete redo of the Wechsler Sweets 1953 books. Those idiots waited for an auditor to catch them to admit they had claimed higher prices for cocoa. The auditor spotted that the money spent for cocoa was too large a fraction of production costs, and from there his job was easy. I told them they would get caught but they wouldn't listen.

Despite his efforts to escape his interest in Shimshon, Hyman could not. His curiosity kept intensifying. When he heard Shimshon speaking in the corridor around eleven Tuesday morning, Hyman listened intently.

"Israel's the place for Jews, Sam. When someone there hates your guts, you can be sure it's personal."

"Take my blessing and go to Israel any time you want," Sam said. "But please stop trying to convince me to move, Shimshon."

"What makes you sure America won't start bothering Jews?"

"Only one person in America regularly bothers this Jew," Sam said. "You. 'Why don't you worry about this, why not worry about that?' "

"Which is exactly what the Jews in Germany said."

"America's not Germany. It's not Hungary. And thank God it's not Israel either. We've got Canadians to the north, Mexicans to the south, and oceans east and west, which I personally prefer to some jihad, or whatever they call it when one hundred million screaming Arabs promise to slaughter you in a holy war."

Sam and Shimshon stopped talking.

Hyman listened to hear whether they would start again. But a few seconds later he heard Sam talking with Abromowitz, saying that the crucial seventh game of the World Series would be played that afternoon. They were talking fast and loudly. Hyman had no interest in the World Series; he realized that Shimshon would not join in this ridiculous American preoccupation. So he went back to work.

He did not appreciate—nor would he have cared—that Tuesday evening, October 4, 1955, was a night that would live forever in Brooklynites' memories. The impossible actually happened. After fifty years, the Brooklyn Dodgers, always the bridesmaid, became the bride; they won their first World Series. All over Brooklyn, in Brighton Beach, Bensonhurst, Boro Park, Flatbush and Sheepshead Bay, in Cobble Hill, Bedford-Stuyvesant, Gerritsen Bay and Park Slope, that night was a Jewish wedding and New Year's Eve wrapped into one. Drunken revelers on New Utrecht and Neptune avenues hugged and kissed. Every bar overflowed. Subway riders on the BMT and IND lines embraced absolute strangers.

Prejudices dropped away. Catholics, Protestants and Jews, blacks, whites and Puerto Ricans (who adopted as their own Sandy Amoros, the Cuban-born left fielder who made the incredible Series-saving catch in the seventh game) hugged one another passionately and jumped up and down in disbelief and ecstasy on Flatbush Avenue. Podres's name was shouted from Canarsie to Brooklyn Heights. Men and women on Atlantic Avenue, Ocean Parkway and under the El near the Boardwalk sang in the streets until dawn; Coney Island celebrated until dawn. People who had met only seconds before locked arms and paraded joyously, singing around the Hotel Bossert where the team members were celebrating the great victory.

The next morning, October fifth, Sam gathered the men together and announced that at one thirty P.M., Lou G. Siegel's restaurant would deliver a catered lunch; a fully stocked bar would be open and, naturally, food and drinks were on the house. A basket of Dodger caps was delivered; all the employees who wanted caps for themselves or for their kids could take as many as they wanted. And the office would close at three. The boss from Brooklyn would celebrate with his troops. And perhaps he would get a few hours' work out of men who wanted to celebrate all day long.

Hyman was incredulous when he heard the news. Close the office early? Was a stupid sports game something you got overjoyed about and let interfere with important work? As usual, Shimshon came by at noon. Hyman ate alone and avoided the celebration. He had to leave when the office closed. But at least the damned World Series was over for a year, he thought.

On Thursday, the office was back to normal, although talk about the Series never stopped. That morning Sam took an office "tour" and stopped at Shimshon's cubicle—two up the corridor from Hyman's—as he did every few days. He chatted about work, left, came one cubicle closer, *kvelled* and checked with Abromowitz.

Sam's parties were not simply generosity; his "tours" were not simply courtesy calls. Naturally, he knew everyone's work. He also knew their families. Sure he could schmooze about Furillo and Hodges, and talk about Snider's longest home run. But as an experienced businessman, he knew what really counted. Sam maintained that the dearest property a boss could possess was an employee's allegiance. Since most people on salary consider their wages an entitlement, a boss who wanted his employees to work enthusiastically had to take a personal interest in their lives. Sam was naturally generous. But he was neither an angel nor a fool. He also had to assure himself that the men and women were being careful. So he visited every accountant's cubicle at least once a week, sometimes more often. Faye checked the secretaries.

When an employee's child had a birthday, the firm sent a card and a five-dollar bill as a present. When a secretary or accountant married, they received a silver teapot or a leaded crystal bowl from Tiffany's. But no matter how often Sam visited others, he came to Hyman's cubicle only every other Friday. They performed a predictable ritual. Sam asked, "Is there anything I could get you?"

Hyman always shook his head no, shifted uneasily in his chair. The boss stared at him, he thought, as if he were viewing a corpse. A few awkward, silent moments passed. Then Sam handed Hyman an envelope filled with one-dollar bills (Hyman wanted to take home nothing larger than ones).

Hyman stuffed the envelope into his pants pocket unopened, said "Thank you, Mr. Teitlebaum" and went back to work.

"Couldn't you use more, Mr. Schwartz?"

"For what?"

"Isn't it high time you rented an apartment?"

"I got everything I need at the Excelsior."

That ended their conversation, unless Hyman needed a few extra dollars for rent or to buy new underwear or socks. Then he would ask Sam to put the additional amount in the next week's envelope.

When Sam was leaving on October seventh, Hyman asked, "That Shimshon said you sent him to me for lessons. He's lying, isn't he?"

"I told him you'd be the best teacher for him. You two have a lot in common."

Hyman had no idea what the boss was referring to. A lot in common wasn't family. It wasn't strangers either. But he was too clever to fall into the boss's trap by inquiring further. He knew that asking meant wanting, and wanting implied needing, and needing invited conversation, which started friendships, which was something Hyman had long ago disavowed.

Chapter Seven

THREE WEEKS AFTER YOM KIPPUR, Sam first checked Shimshon's worksheets and was surprised. For a newcomer's, they were careful and accurate. Sam wanted to compliment him, but with Shimshon proselytizing about Israel constantly, he got no opportunity. Shimshon insisted that all good Jews should emigrate.

"You think like a ghetto Jew, Sam. Maybe your children—"

"Maybe my children will go to Columbia, not to CCNY. But tell me Shimshon. Is there anything you're not expert at?"

"Accounting."

"At least there's something I'm better at, although I've begun to wonder how long that distinction will last."

"Wonder no more. Teach me and find out. And I'll teach you Hebrew. Listen, Sam—"

"Here we go again. 'If you were really smart you'd leave everything, move to a kibbutz and transform yourself into a peasant.' " He put his hand on Shimshon's shoulder. "Let me tell you something, Shimson. Jews don't belong on farms. They belong in cafés." Sam straightened up. "I hire a student, and I get a spiritual advisor. You're really something." Sam playfully pinched Shimshon's cheek. Then he smiled approvingly. "You're really something."

Shimshon was not always so enthusiastic. One morning later in October he told Sam, "Hyman says the same damned thing every day: 'I eat alone!' "

"Sometimes, you try something and can't succeed. If Hyman wants to be left alone, why not learn from Abromowitz?"

"He can't teach me to be excellent. You're the one who said Hyman needs someone."

"That was before Jack Rossberg told me that right after Kol Nidre night's Kaddish, Hyman started screaming that God was a monster who killed his family. He caused such a commotion they had to carry him out."

"Our little Hyman caused a commotion?"

"Our little Hyman is nuts! Jack's not one to exaggerate." Sam pointed to the plaque with its ornate Yiddish letters: I never judge a man who had to be where I did not. "Those words are Jack's. He considers himself damned lucky to have gotten here. In 1938 he paid rates higher than first class to stow away on the *Normandy*. For a week he ate moldy bread and shat in a pail. But he got here. By the time the war ended, he had built a big dress factory. I did lots of work for him and he never complained about the bill. One day he told me that a new business was opening—the immigrant business. He had volunteered me as a founding partner. After that, a new bag of bones came here every few weeks. Jack took even more.

"We became closer friends. One afternoon we were laughing about the market, sipping twelve-year-old Chivas, when Jack stopped short. 'I have a hard time enjoying myself lately,' he said and put down his glass. 'The world's upside-down. Men who were Herr Professors at the University of Heidelberg and industrialists in Cracow stop *me* on Thirty-eighth Street just to say 'Excuse me, sir. I hope I'm not bothering you, but, please. Please let me thank you for bringing me here.' I have to force myself to look them in the eye. If I went through what they did, I doubt I could live again."

"Cut it out. People adapt," Shimshon interjected nervously.

"Learn a thing or two from Jack, like humility and compassion. That afternoon he told me, 'I'll never judge a man who had to be where I did not.' I inscribed those words on plaques for Jack and me. He lives those words. Unfortunately, I only aspire to them."

"What does that have to do with Hyman?"

"Those words are why I try not to see what Hyman did to his clothes. They're why you should have realized by now that Hyman isn't exactly jumping up and down over your visits."

"Do you really want me to give up?"

Sam nodded.

"That's because to you he's more dead than alive." Shimshon stood. "But I know that guy. He's just like a hundred other crabby old Jewish men. He pushes me away and is so particular. Whenever he says he never studied accounting, he emphasizes *accounting* to make sure you don't think he never studied anything."

Sam glanced at the rows of well-cared-for leatherbound books on his office wall, so different from yeshiva Talmuds, whose bindings were always cracked and whose pages were always all but erased by wear. Hyman's work suggested that he had probably studied something mathematical. Yet Sam could not remember ever having seen Hyman carrying a book or reading a newspaper. "Hyman may have studied Talmud," Sam said. "But he studied secular subjects as well."

"What makes you so sure?"

"Has Abromowitz ever played 'How fast can you count in your head' with you?"

"No."

"It starts when Abromowitz snaps out two numbers and a function. Like three hundred forty-six, nine hundred twenty-seven—multiply. No paper or pencils allowed. Only in your head. Whoever answers first, wins. As the prize,

Abromowitz brings the winner a cinnamon doughnut the next morning. One lunchtime in 1949, Abromowitz threw out two numbers and before he had even finished saying 'multiply,' they heard a voice from outside the conference room growl out the answer. They looked at one another, not believing that any man could compute that fast. That voice was Hyman's."

"But Abromowitz makes fun of Hyman."

"That's when he started to. The next morning Abromowitz brought the cinnamon doughnut—he calls it 'the winner's circle'—to Hyman's cubicle. Whatever else Abromowitz tells you, he respects a good mind, even one that in his opinion is not one hundred percent there. He congratulated Hyman and asked him how he could figure so fast. Hyman wouldn't take the doughnut. But something finally must have clicked in him, because instead of staying quiet after Abromowitz asked him for the second time how he figured so fast, Hyman said, 'Knowing calculus and number theory don't hurt.' Abromowitz still was upset, and by next morning he was calling Hyman 'that *meshugenah*.' From the way Hyman dresses and acts you'd never guess he had that kind of knowledge."

"But you think he's an educated man."

"He didn't learn calculus in yeshiva."

Chapter Eight

SHIMSHON RETURNED to Hyman's cubicle every day. As time went by, he detected a gradual change. By late October Hyman would swivel around the moment Shimshon arrived each day. Shimshon was almost certain he heard a playful inflection when Hyman said *"mamzer."* But every time Shimshon suggested they eat lunch together, Hyman stopped talking and returned to work.

Matters remained static until November first, a day when dark clouds churned in the sky. Icy gusts outside Teitlebaum & Sharfenstein burrowed through shrunken window grouting and left winter's calling card, a frosted crystalline film on the glass's inner surface.

Shimshon rubbed his thumbnail across the film and lifted off a tiny lump of white snow. He licked it sensuously. Crystals dissolving on his tongue reminded him of Budapest in winter. On cold days its people laced up their boots almost to their knees, pulled on heavy woolen sweaters and bundled themselves inside thick, calf-length coats. Unless fierce storms plundered the city and blackened the streets, no matter how cold the night, families on both sides of the ice-filled Danube strolled elegant gaslit boulevards, chatting and making sure, as the old Hungarian saying goes, that they saw their neighbors and were seen. To enrich winter's bleakness, every pastry shop, café, and restaurant put a crystal vase holding a tiny red rosebud on each table. In Budapest everyone, not just the aristocrats, resisted winter and fought its gloom with color, luxury, hot mineral baths and conversation.

Hyman was some contrast to that! He hardly ever talked, wouldn't eat or drink with anyone, and wore rags that belonged on a vagrant. Shimshon knew that Hyman chose to look disheveled. After all, Hyman made a good living. And that Shimshon could neither comprehend nor tolerate.

On November second, rather than going to Hyman's cubicle at twelve, Shimshon waited until everyone else had gone to the conference room for lunch and the entire office was silent. When Shimshon came to Hyman's cubicle, he found Hyman facing the doorjamb looking befuddled. But the moment Hyman saw him, he bent down as if looking for something he had dropped.

"Worried I wouldn't come by?" Shimshon said.

"Like darkness worries for the moon."

"Darkness is going to teach the moon today. Today you're going to teach me what makes Hyman Schwartz so special."

"Special?" Hyman sat up and smiled sardonically. "I've never thought of myself as special. Let's just say I've visited some special places."

"That's what makes you familiar, Hyman."

"So it's Hyman you call me? Well, you're absolutely right. You're as familiar to me as sweetness is to horseradish. So now that you know how familiar you are, why not make yourself just that scarce?"

Shimshon's smile looked like an arrogant smirk to Hyman. He felt infuriated. "You say you want to learn something?" Hyman stood, pulled up his left sleeve, and held his forearm in front of Shimshon's face. "Do those numbers look familiar?"

"Very, Hyman. It's sticking them under my nose that's unusual."

Hyman lowered his arm and said nothing.

"I've seen your tattoo every day for the last month. You weren't exactly subtle about it."

Hyman's face turned blood-red.

"Only one thing surprised me. How you show it off."

Hyman shuddered; his glasses slid down his nose. His body shook, his rage barely controlled. "Get the hell out of here. You got respect for nothing."

As Hyman pushed up his glasses, he remembered a day when the commandant had strutted into the barracks. Everyone stood ramrod straight. But Cohen's glasses slid so far down the sweat on his nose that he had to push them up. The commandant caught sight of the movement. He carefully lifted off Cohen's glasses, lay them delicately on the floor, and shattered their thick lenses under his heel. "Put them on, *Jude*," he smiled. "Now that they're lighter, they won't fall off." After the commandant left, Cohen collapsed on his group's bunk, wearing bent, empty rims, saying over and over, "Why steal what you can't give back?" Five minutes later they took him to the gas.

"You still don't recognize *mishpucha?*" Shimshon was saying.

"Stupid God kills fine boys and lets bastards live?"

"God, schmod." Shimshon stood up straight. "If you really want to get rid of me today, you'll have to throw me out."

Hyman clenched his fists in front of him.

Shimshon came one step closer and smirked provocatively.

"You're asking for a fight," Hyman said. He knew there had to be a time when a man says "no more," a time when even dying doesn't matter.

Shimshon rolled up his left shirtsleeve and dropped his arms to his side. "All I need to fight you is one arm, and not even my right one. You go first, Hyman. Let's see if you have the guts to hit me."

Hyman saw a small boy's hand waving good-bye to his papa. The smell of Buna's ashes seared his nostrils. Punch that bastard's jaw, punch it for David and Rachel. Punch it for Gittel and Yankelah. Punch it for Cohen's glasses. Punch it for faces with no names, for voices without people. Use your fists, Hyman Schwartz. You looked Death in the eye and didn't flinch. Draw blood. Kill that son of a bitch.

"So," Shimshon said.

Hyman caught Shimshon off guard. He smashed Shimshon's mouth with a blow from his right fist and split his lip. Shimshon backed away. He wiped off the blood. "Very good, Mr. Schwartz. But aren't you alive enough to punch harder?"

"God, I'm going to kill you." Hyman punched again. This time Shimshon grabbed Hyman's wrists, and held them both in his large right hand. Hyman tried to free himself. But Shimshon held him tightly.

"If you're alive, Mr. Schwartz, you must be open to facts. Punch bastards, not someone who's like family to you."

Hyman struggled to free his hands, but Shimshon's grip held. "Your turn, you stinking bastard," Hyman said, his teeth clenched. "Punch me. Hit me hard. You can't break me anymore."

Shimshon lifted his left arm.

Hyman turned away to stop the punch he anticipated from catching him face-on.

But Shimshon said, "Take a look. See something familiar."

Out of the corner of his eyes Hyman saw a few colored spots. In the midst of blood streaks, freckles and auburn hairs, an A and four blue numbers were tattooed on Shimshon's forearm.

"I saw my father throw himself on the fence," Shimshon said. "You look like a man who knows what it feels like to see the people you love die in front of your eyes."

"In front of your eyes?" Hyman mumbled.

"You lost and I lost. That makes us almost family in a European sort of way, doesn't it?" Shimshon said, letting go of Hyman's wrists. "Now do you understand?"

Hyman slumped into his chair. *In front of your eyes?* Dazed, he stared at the curls framing Shimshon's face. Is that how David would have looked? Would he have grown up big and strong, a man who wouldn't flinch if someone punched him?

Hyman walked wordlessly past Shimshon and returned a moment later carrying a folding chair. "Please, please," he said, opening the chair beside his desk. "Please." He motioned for Shimshon to sit.

Hyman ate very little that day. But he invited Shimshon back for the next day's lunch. By the following noon, not only had Hyman regained his appetite, but he brought a Horn & Hardart sandwich for Shimshon as well.

Chapter Nine

"PLEASE. PLEASE," Hyman had said, his mind filled with questions. Please tell me Shimshon. Am I the only one who never sleeps at night? Do you yearn so desperately for your woman that just to stay alive you count numbers in your head? Do you watch your legs walking and your fingers working and your chest breathing and still have too little evidence to know whether you're alive or dead? And then do you realize you're not sure because you don't know which you'd prefer? What's the use of moving your fingers if everything's gone? Why are you alive? Maybe you should be gone too, ashes like them? Have you forgiven God, Shimshon? Maybe you have less to forgive Him for. You're too young to have had a wife or to wonder whether you should have been home so you could have died trying to save your son.

Then other questions came. What would David have looked like now? Would he be tall, handsome, and clever? Would he have a good mind and a warm heart? Or would he have turned out to be a small, scared man like his papa?

Hyman and Shimshon ate lunch together the next workday too. Hyman spoke very little, but Shimshon gabbled on and on about how badly he wanted to learn every aspect of accounting. He didn't want Hyman to think he was a neophyte. After all, he had been the best apprentice in the whole Hungarian Central Economic Ministry. But since

Shimshon wanted to be a full-fledged autonomous accountant who knew how to keep books that reflected actual numbers instead of what Communist governments call reality, he needed to know more. "When will the lessons begin?" he asked over and over again. "When will the lessons begin?"

Hyman heard himself inviting Shimshon to a fourth lunch. He realized that although Shimshon obviously relished the invitation, he seemed to be forcing himself to finish the sandwich. For the first time, Hyman paid attention to what he had been eating every day since landing in New York. The white bread tasted like sawdust, the lettuce was wilted and the chicken in the sandwiches was meat flecks held together by gelatin.

Since Hyman had extended the invitation, he had taken on an obligation. And when Hyman Schwartz committed himself to a job, he always did it perfectly. The food he brought Shimshon had to improve. Since late 1945, he had passed an orange neon sign near Thirty-third Street every day. It spelled FLIEGEL AND PULKA'S DELICATESSEN. Hyman had never had any urge to enter before.

But the next morning, after pausing near the door to gather his courage, he stepped into the crowded delicatessen. Aromas of onion, garlic, and paprika on roasting chickens greeted and overwhelmed him. They triggered sensations too painful to remember yet too wonderful to forget. Hyman felt as if he had walked into his Warsaw apartment on Sabbath eve. Entranced, he stood inside, envisioning Rachel circling the tall white candles with her hands, saying Sabbath eve prayers. *"Bo-wee. Bo-wee. Shabat Hamalkah."* Come be with us, Bride of the Sabbath. Let your white lace gown flow through our door and your bejeweled tiara light up our home.

Every few moments, Hyman saw a hand at the delicatessen's front reach up and pull a chain that clicked a machine on the wall one number higher. "Number forty-four. Next. Forty-four," a voice called out, and a customer thrust forward a Formica tag. Hyman stood on his toes, eager to see what was happening up there. But the crowd was too high and dense for a short man to see above. "Number forty-five next," a second voice called out. "Number forty-six." Hyman realized that the delicatessen also used numbers to bring order from chaos. He fought his way through a sea of woolen overcoats, Stetsons, slouch hats, and caps and made it to the side, where he took plastic tag number 67 off a hook.

Delicious aromas filled the air. Five minutes later Hyman was nearer the front. Through tweeds and weaves in front of him, he discerned light glinting off a straight piece of stainless steel and two glass panes.

"Next. Number fifty-two. Next."

"Next. Number fifty-three. Next."

As numbers were served and customers left, Hyman got close enough to see that the stainless steel and glass were the front of a long case behind which two middle-aged men and a young Puerto Rican rushed to fill orders. The frenzied activity was so different from the Automat's sterile efficiency. But what overwhelmed Hyman was the food. In contrast to the neatly wrapped sandwiches and spotted fruit inside the Automat's tiny glass vaults, the metal bowls, bins, hooks and broilers at Fliegel and Pulka's overflowed with appetizing, succulent food.

Rectangular, stainless-steel bowls brimmed over with chicken salad, tuna salad and chopped chicken liver. There were bowls with herring (schmaltz or matjes), and others with cream cheese, Swiss, Muenster and American cheese, and a small wooden tub filled with cottage cheese. Roast beef, corned beef, tongue, pastrami, turkey meat white and dark, and Nova Scotia lox were piled in high stacks. Sliced Bermuda and Spanish onions, black, green and brown Greek olives, crisp iceberg lettuce leaves, and slices of ripe tomatoes filled other bowls.

Wire bins pressed flush against the store's plate-glass front window were filled with onion rolls, French rolls and bagels (plain, poppy, salt and onion); another bin was filled with loaves: white breads and long ryes (plain and with seeds, both in brown and white varieties) and a long loaf of pumpernickel so dark that it looked like crumbly black soil. Suspended above the bins on clusters of silver hooks were smoked and processed meats: salamis, long and short, dried and fresh, and two pale pink bolognas.

Three wooden barrels were set against the wall behind the counter, so that the men filling orders had to weave around them. One barrel was filled with dark green half-sour pickles, the second with olive-green all-sours, and the third with crisp white sauerkraut. Then Hyman saw where the sizzling sound had come from. A tall broiler down near the wall farthest from the window glowed electric-fire-orange and roasted more than thirty chickens on six slowly-rotating spits.

"Number sixty, next," one of the men said. LOU PULKA was embroidered on his apron. "Number sixty-one. Okay Art. You get sixty-two." Then 63, 64 and 65 were served.

Hyman had never seen so much food since coming to New York. Nor had he cared to. But now that he had decided to bring lunch for Shimshon, he would do his job perfectly and buy food that would thrill the palate of even a brash young newcomer.

"Sixty-six. Next, number sixty-six," Mr. Pulka shouted. Hyman now stood right in front of the glass case.

The other man, Art Fliegel, who looked like a cherub wearing a Dodgers cap, lay a fresh lettuce leaf and three slices of tomato on top of 65's tuna, closed the sandwich, and wrapped it in sandwich paper. When he finished, he wiped his hands on his white butcher's apron and took the customer's money. Then he clicked the machine one number higher. "Number sixty-seven. Next. Sixty-seven," he said.

Hyman handed his plastic tag to Mr. Fliegel. "Maybe you make sandwiches from the chickens?"

"Do we make chicken sandwiches? How many do you want? Ten? A hundred? A thousand?"

"All I want is two."

"Two chicken sandwiches on what kind of bread?"

48

Hyman shrugged his shoulders. He had not figured out sandwich-buying to that level of detail.

"Trust Art to take care of you." Fliegel went to the rotisserie and brought back half a chicken. The aroma wafting past almost made Hyman faint. Fliegel placed the chicken on the long wooden cutting board. "You got two chicken on onion coming up." He sliced open two onion rolls. The aroma of onions, burned until they were shriveled brown flakes, filled the air. Fliegel spread mayonnaise on both open rolls, slid the succulent meat off the bones and distributed it evenly on the rolls. He put a lettuce leaf and a few slices of tomato on top of each and pressed the sandwiches closed, wrapping them in heavy white paper.

"From your accent I can tell you're a Galizianer, mister. Trust Art to know what else Galizianers like." Fliegel leaned into the all-sour pickle barrel and straightened up waving a large pickle in each hand. "Like life. Bitter as hell but delicious all the same." Drops of brine dripped off as Fliegel wrapped each pickle in its own aluminum foil.

He rang up the bill and asked Hyman for three dollars and sixty cents.

Three dollars and sixty cents, Hyman thought, watching Fliegel making change for his four ones. He charges the same for delicacies as the Automat charges for dreck. Hyman started to leave, but Fliegel called after him. "Be sure to come back, mister. Remember. Fliegel and Pulka's serves what Galizianers like."

Chapter Ten

HYMAN'S EARS TURNED RED in the strong wind outside; his exhalations transformed into cloudpuffs. Although cold seeped through his overcoat's weave, he felt warm. The aroma of onion, garlic and paprika had reminded him of home. The eternity that had passed since he had lost his family no longer existed. For a moment he was sure that now everything would be perfect. In his mind he pictured David leaning against Rachel's side, peering into the oven to check whether the Sabbath eve chicken was ready. He crossed Thirty-second and Thirty-first streets astonished. Warmth and delicacy were back. Wait till Shimshon smells these sandwiches, he thought. Wait till he tastes these pickles!

In a dreamworld of flawless diamonds where each happenstance is a preordained facet of the perfect grand scheme, Hyman reached Thirtieth Street certain that Shimshon would be there waiting. When he was not, Hyman circled the block to give him time. But Shimshon still had not arrived when Hyman returned to Thirtieth Street. Perplexed, disbelieving that this gem could be flawed too, Hyman shook his head and stepped off the curb.

But a gust lifted his hat and skittered it down Thirtieth Street. "Come back you," Hyman shouted, turning and rushing after it. He picked up the hat. "I got to keep tabs on you every minute. If I don't the next thing I know you'll run off and get yourself killed." Delicately, he brushed the street grit off its brim. "Be careful from now on. I don't want to see you run over."

Precisely at eight, Hyman came to the office and went to his cubicle. Nimble with procedures, playful with calculations, he felt like the mathematician Professor Minkowski had said an accountant could never be. Aromas and recollections had gotten him to consider teaching. But he was still a sober man with doubts. Bringing a sandwich to say you're sorry is reparations; teaching subjects as complex as depreciation and a Victor adding machine's rhythm is a commitment. A boy who can't come to work on time won't learn. He'll race in here late and out of breath. "Teach me quickly," he'll say. "Hurry, Mr. Schwartz. I can only stay a short while. I have to run to my next adventure." Shimshon's the kind of boy who's always running.

Shimshon is the kind of boy . . . In the minutes before noon on Friday Hyman thought for the first time of Shimshon as a human. Not "Mr. Just Shimshon," not "a chameleon," not "you little *mamzer*," not some floating face no different than two eyes and a smile painted on cardboard, not some time warp here to make reparations but a real flesh-and-blood person who worked at Teitlebaum & Sharfenstein. Shimshon, he thought. He's just a boy. But if my David came to a strange place, wouldn't I wish someone would teach him? Where is that kid?

As St. Anne's tolled, Shimshon appeared at the doorjamb carrying a folding chair. "May I, Mr. Schwartz?" Shimshon opened the chair.

"To eat we need a clean table," Hyman said and cleared the desk. He sprayed the top with Windex and polished the glass until it sparkled. Then he handed Shimshon the sandwich.

Shimshon unwrapped it and looked at the sandwich with appreciative eyes. He licked its side. Aromas of fresh dough, burnt onions and roast chicken scented the air. "Is this from a different store?"

"A man goes to lots of stores," Hyman said handing Shimshon a pickle. "Do Hungarians like their pickles all-sour?"

"Do we?" Shimshon closed his eyes and bit into the pickle. Aromas of dill, garlic and vinegar permeated the air. "Do we!" His face broke into a broad smile.

Hyman had purchased food he hoped would please Shimshon. Although he himself ate little of his sandwich and pickle, he scrutinized Shimshon's reactions. Did he chew the pickle slowly? Did he smile like David used to when he got his favorite foods? Was Shimshon like Papa, who used to scrunch a burnt onion between his front teeth to savor it?

Shimshon's obvious pleasure reassured Hyman. He decided to do it. "Eat fast if you want to learn," he said.

Shimshon did not seem surprised. "I knew you'd teach me, I just knew you would."

Hyman had expected a more excited reaction. But he was not really disappointed. As he watched Shimshon quietly enjoying every bite, he was on the verge of shivering. How starved have you been? he thought, because Shimshon seemed to have no sense that seconds and minutes were passing. Who's taken care of you, young man? When Hyman glanced at his watch, it was twelve forty. "It's late. We'll begin lessons Monday."

"No." Shimshon gobbled his sandwich and chugged the water. "Let's start now. At least teach me one lesson today."

"If you insist, I'll teach you the most important one." Hyman cleared his desk. He sprayed and polished each grease spot until the glass top gleamed.

"Start already," Shimshon said. "I really want to learn."

"Okay. The most important thing for an accountant to know is who is the enemy."

"The enemy?"

"Yeah, the enemy, the accountant's cancer, the big M. Mistakes. Only one medicine kills it. Meticulousness. Check every computation at least three times before you make it a final entry." Because Shimshon looked confused, Hyman stopped. "Bring Acme Leather's worksheet on Monday. We'll look through it for simple mistakes. Then you'll understand."

"I'm not without experience."

Hyman glanced at the glass surface, checking whether it was spotless. "Experience and meticulousness don't necessarily go hand in hand."

"My work is careful. What will you teach me after you see how meticulous I am?"

Hyman shook his head. "Then I'll teach you the corollary, the second most important rule of accounting."

"Which is?"

"I told you already," Hyman said, respraying a grease spot. "To eat faster."

"I don't want to ruin what's delicious. But what will you teach when you see that I already avoid mistakes?"

"That what you understand is true for eating is also the fundamental rule of work." Hyman looked directly at Shimshon. "The next lesson in accounting is learning an art."

"An art?"

The bells tolled twelve forty-five.

"Yeah, an art," Hyman said. "How not to rush."

Chapter Eleven

AS ALWAYS, Hyman spent most of the weekend in his room and the rest of it traveling. On Sunday morning, to prove to himself how well he knew New York, he put on his spare shirt, his extra pair of slacks and the dilapidated green overcoat he had come to America in and rode the BMT Brighton Line to Coney Island. Hyman anticipated each subway stop. After Avenue J comes Avenue M, on the Brighton Beach local of course. Hyman was very proud to be expert on subways; he could go anywhere in New York without checking a map or asking for directions.

At six A.M. on Monday morning, he picked up his workday clothes at Wong Fat's, returned to the Excelsior to change and went to work. At noon, Shimshon came to the doorway carrying a chair and a worksheet in one hand and a Gristede's supermarket bag in the other. He stepped into the cubicle, opened the bag and put two glasses, a large bottle of tomato juice, two bananas and a few plums on the polished desktop.

"Did you leave hungry Friday?" Hyman said.

"Are you kidding? But if you do the teaching, I at least want to do something for you."

"For me you can learn." Although Hyman was curt, the colors that the food had dappled on his desk startled and pleased him. The tomato juice was deep red, the onion rolls were honey-brown. The pickles were actually olive-green, the plums were dark purple, and the yellow bananas were speckled with cocoa-colored spots. Under the fluorescent lights, even the grease stains on the white wrapping paper glistened like black mother-of-pearl.

For the first time since the war Hyman really enjoyed food. The juice was cold, silty, almost thick enough to chew. "This is good," he said softly. "I'll bring food. You have my permission to bring an extra or two."

"Don't forget to start teaching me today."

"I may be old, young man, but I'm not senile. Did you forget that we started Friday? When we finish lunch, we'll go further."

Between bites, Shimshon spoke. "You know, after the war, my mother and I hoped that the new government would be kind to Jews. When the Communists came to power in the late forties and Rákosi headed the government, even after his government began to nationalize businesses we figured life would be better for us. After all, Rákosi was a Jewish tailor's son. And at first Rákosi's group was good to us. But later, as soon as Hungary had economic trouble, the good-old anti-Semitism started again and Jews were blamed. Like termites in wood, some infestations are just too ingrown to get rid of. It's strange, though. I still miss Budapest some-times. Do you ever miss Europe, Mr. Schwartz?"

Hyman shrugged his shoulders and continued chewing his pickle. Shimshon took the cue, decided he had better not upset Hyman, and asked no further questions. As soon as they had finished lunch, Hyman asked Shimshon to clear the desk; he sprayed and polished it. Hyman sat in front of his adding machine, entered a number and pulled the long han-dle; thin paper racheted one notch higher. He put in a second number, pulled the handle twice, hunched over the machine to examine the sum.

"Perfect," Hyman said and looked relaxed. "My Victor has been perfectly dependable for years. But I still don't take chances. I check him each morning and after every lunch. Do the same with yours." Hyman swiveled to face Shimshon. "Let's see your worksheet from Acme."

For the the rest of that lunch and during every lunch until late November, Hyman reviewed Shimshon's worksheets. He told him a dozen times to be more careful, insisted repeatedly that Shimshon enter numbers so that worksheet columns were straight as a ruler, even taught him a technique to keep balances that you were still working on, running balances. Hyman restricted their conversations to worksheets, ledgers and errors. Although the topic was limited, accounting and numbers were Hyman's life; his sharing them was a revelation. "Don't ever forget," Hyman said. "Mistakes are the enemy. A man who keeps lousy books will always be a lousy accountant."

Chapter Twelve

IN CENTRAL PARK, maples that had blazed gold, orange and red in early November had been humbled and turned leafless by the month's fourth week. Although icy winds were swooping down from Canada, Hyman felt invigorated. Shimshon had stopped trying to talk about personal things, which left Hyman freer to teach. Good teaching started with fundamentals and built on them.

"All final entries should be in pen," Hyman taught.

"Why?"

"Because pencil can be erased. If your debits and credits don't match, one day some fancy-Dan auditor will look at you suspiciously. And when he talks to Mr. Teitlebaum, he'll stumble over words, making believe that it's hard for him to let on what he's thinking. After the boss has encouraged him—'You can tell me'—the auditor will suggest, reluctantly of course, that you might just be a crook."

Shimshon looked puzzled, as if asking, "Why?"

"To an auditor, catching a crooked accountant is life's pinnacle."

"And a pen is going to stop him?"

"Of course pen will stop him. You can't erase it."

"You still have to change mistakes."

"If you make them! The first rule is not to. But if you

haven't been meticulous, accountants use a standard convention. Cross out the old number with a single stroke, enter the correct one to the right and put down the date and your initials. Always initial everything you do. Your initials tell whoever checks that you take full responsibility."

Shimshon smiled and gathered together his papers. "You think of everything, Mr. Schwartz."

Hyman mumbled as Shimshon disappeared around the doorframe. "I should be so lucky. I should be so lucky."

On November 21, Sam knocked on Shimshon's doorjamb. "Well look who's here," Shimshon said. "The stranger."

"With the teaching you're getting you don't need me."

"You, I don't need, Sam Teitlebaum. You I like."

"Me, you like to drive crazy. But Mildred convinced me we got off cheap on Yom Kippur. How about joining us for Thanksgiving dinner, the real McCoy American holiday?"

"Name your time."

"Noon, Thursday. You know the way by train." Sam hesitated. "I still can't believe you got Hyman to teach you. He turned me down for Thanksgiving dinner, which keeps his streak perfect at ten in a row. How did you do it?"

Shimshon's hands made prestidigitator's circles in the air. "We are capable of the impossible."

"Don't take Hyman lightly, Shimshon."

"Lightly? I got him to teach me."

"You've performed a miracle. But that man has a volcano inside. I don't want it erupting."

"Why do you underestimate him?"

"I hold Hyman Schwartz in my highest esteem. But I've learned to accept who he is."

"You wanted him to teach me."

"I never thought you'd get anywhere so I never thought through my suggestion. He's a brittle guy. Don't push him any farther or faster than he can go." Sam started to leave. "And don't forget our Thursday date. Mildred is planning a first-class Thanksgiving. Turkey, stuffing, cranberry sauce,

58

yams, the works. Bring your appetite. We'll make a Yankee out of you yet."

Shimshon was surprised by Sam's naïveté. A man had to be iron to survive a concentration camp. No weaklings survived hell. Hyman Schwartz was plenty tough.

The Wednesday before Thanksgiving was very cold. Ominous clouds threatened to bury the city under snow. Everyone rushed to finish work early and get home before the first precipitation. At lunch, Hyman said that it was time to serve food for thought. "Today I want to raise a fundamental question. What's a decimal point?"

Since Hyman seemed to be loosening up, Shimshon kidded. "A decimal point is a tenth of a point. And a millipoint is a thousandth."

"Don't joke with me. If I didn't consider the question fundamental, I wouldn't ask it."

"All right. All right. A decimal point separates the dollars from the cents."

"Most people would say that you're absolutely correct. But you're correct in only a specialized sense. For our purposes, where Victor places his decimal point is arbitrary."

"Not true. Decimal points always separate pennies from dollars."

"If you think simplistically, which doesn't become you, young man. What you say is certainly true for final records. But for intermediate steps it's better to say that adding machines print decimal points in an arbitrary place. Do you see how crucial knowing that is?"

Shimshon had no idea what Hyman was driving at.

"Why do I waste my time on you?" Hyman said.

"I'm a challenge. Can an imbecile be taught?"

"I've seen plenty of imbeciles and you're not one of them. But you're so afraid to let go of what some bookkeeper in Budapest told you that you can't learn how to think."

"I'm afraid?" Shimshon said. "Look who's talking."

"Who's talking is the man who slaved two whole years to learn accounting's basics. So what's a decimal point?"

Shimshon shrugged his shoulders.

"If Victor decides where the decimal point is, he always chooses two spaces from the right," Hyman said. "Right?"

Shimshon nodded.

"Which means that Victor will make every number exact give or take a penny. As long as I never multiply or divide that's exact enough. But even in basic bookkeeping I divide and multiply. If I want to be exact to the mil or decimil, I have to change Victor's natural ways. Which is why I'm asking you what a decimal point is."

"Are you saying that Victor can be made more accurate?"

"Miracles of miracles." Hyman held up his hands as if offering hosannas. "He can think." He leaned toward Shimshon. "No law says I have to accept Victor's decision. If I make the decimal point three or four spaces from the right and stay consistent, I can make Victor ten, a hundred, a thousand, even ten thousand times more accurate. Now do you understand?"

Shimshon nodded lackadaisically.

"Today you think, 'Mr. Schwartz is crazy meticulous.' Don't deny it. I can see what you're thinking. After the first time you spend weeks reviewing two-year-old calculations because you multiplied seven products of sloppy divisions by a hundred thousand, you'll wish you'd learned to use decimal points to advantage. Ask Goldstein.

"Go. Go. Go ask him, big shot. When the government decided to audit one of Goldstein's accounts, he spent two entire weeks hunting for stupid mistakes. The government suspected that Trinity Slacks was a bunch of crooks and was doing one of their extra-special audits. At first, nice Mr. Teitlebaum dropped by every few hours, just to check, you know. 'Do they balance yet?'

"For the three days before the audit Mr. Teitlebaum sat shoulder-to-shoulder with Goldstein going through two-year-old books line by line, looking for every wrong multiplication. There were plenty. Mr. Teitlebaum is a lot nicer when you don't lose him money. A fraction on zippers, a few mil on buttons, three more on cuffs, and four on belt loops multiplied by three hundred thousand trousers can be a major scandal to a man with an army contract. How would you like to sweat through twenty shirts in two weeks, Mr. Tisza?"

"If they take two years to figure it out, it won't be my problem. But I would hate to cause Sam heartburn."

"If they're your books, it's your problem."

"Two years from now I'll be in Israel."

Although that news was old, Hyman was shocked. He could not figure out why he was upset that Shimshon would leave someday. Rather than looking at Shimshon's face, he stared at the empty, red-streaked juice glasses, the crumb-filled sandwich paper, the banana peels browning on their exposed surfaces. He glanced at Shimshon's star of David, then followed the arch of red curls surrounding his face. "A man can never know where he'll be in two years. But one thing is true now and will be true forever: Being careful never hurts. Because then your ledgers will balance down to the last penny."

Hyman was glad when Shimshon left. He found himself wondering whether Shimshon had the perseverance to complete his education. But he reassured himself that Shimshon's ultimate plans were no concern of his. Yet the afternoon went slowly. And at dinner that evening, Horn & Hardart's food disgusted him. The turkey was dry; the yams tasted like glue. For almost ten years their food had been perfectly adequate. Why now did it taste like ashes? Later, Hyman was dissatisfied with his room. For two months he had washed his face only in the shower because when he looked at his sink, he remembered piss running down its sides. That's how it begins, he thought. And before you know it, you're drinking it and enjoying it like the walking dead of Buna. His body stiffened; he scratched his forearm and raised welts.

Stop remembering. Two times 12 is 24 and how much is

2,999 times 15,002? It's 44,990,998, of course. That's easy. You're using 99s again. Go to hard figures. But Hyman's thoughts would not disappear. I've got a room of my own and a boss who gives me the best seat in the house. Why did Shimshon come to disturb me? Or did God send him as an apology? Should I bow down and say, "Thank You, thank You, good God?" Do You think I'm Job? You send a replacement and everything's back to normal? "No," Hyman said out loud. People aren't numbers and that *mamzer*'s not my son. Send my David back!

Lost in thought, Hyman settled into his maroon velvet armchair and looked out the window. The moon was high. In the light cast out by his window, occasional snowflakes drifted down and twinkled like sequins.

Leaning against the chilly window, Hyman watched the Boulevard Hotel's orange sign turn on and off and saw Broadway's streetlights change from red to green. Since his first day here, Hyman had been fascinated by the sign just across Fifty-eighth Street. Illuminated by light from the almost-full moon, the faded billboard portrayed a side of beef. Its right side said, ABELMAN'S MEATS. SINCE 1905.

Beef. Chicken. What's happening? Lately I taste Fliegel and Pulka's chickens and think about how good our apartment smelled on Sabbath eve. My fingers remember running through Rachel's hair, my mouth tastes her sweet kisses and my penis gets excited because I can feel her hugging me tighter and moving with me when I was inside. Our house smelled good, Rachel smelled good, the whole world bloomed in those years.

Hyman looked at the sign across Fifty-eighth Street. Life always gets colder. Don't fool yourself. You did enough of that on the road back. Then you learned how different 1945's Warsaw was from the one where you held her and made sweet love. Remember what the apartment was like when you came home?

Chapter Thirteen

TEN YEARS had passed since then. No. Ten years and two months. Alone on this day when the entire country was celebrating the New World's abundance and good fortune, Hyman stared blankly out at Manhattan. He leaned back in his chair, clasped his hands tightly and withdrew into a time and place all his own. It was 1945. Europe had been liberated and he was heading north on a farm road on his way to Warsaw. The countryside was desolated; farmland was cratered and rock-strewn. Tank-tread marks and burned-out vehicles were everywhere. Trees that had lined the road were toppled; gnarled, mud-covered roots scratched at the air like arthritic fingers.

Hunger was his constant companion. When the biting pains became ferocious, Hyman scoured every field he passed for a promising patch of soil. He had to risk getting caught and bludgeoned. Polish partisans were rumored to be killing leftover Jews. But what choice did he have? Vigilant for signs of danger, he dug his fingers into clumped soil hoping to unearth a turnip or a potato.

How many larders, broken cabinets and abandoned farmhouses did you explore hoping to discover an unopened tin? he thought, shivering. What would you have given for Horn & Hardart's or a safe bed on those evenings? Hyman remembered huddling beside boulders. One night he had slept inside a windmill, listening all night as its blades' tattered cloth flapped in the wind.

On his tenth day out of Buna, Hyman had spotted a man harnessed to a wooden plow. The man pulled as his wife strained to guide the plow's upcurved arms so that his struggling against its leather straps would, through her guidance, carve furrows in reluctant, battered soil. He fell; she fell. Hyman wondered whether they were mad for trying to prepare soil for spring. Can effort alone revivify exhausted land? They must have been believers, because the man and his wife stood up. He replaced the yoke around his neck, and again pulled stubbornly. She stumbled and fell. But they got up and kept struggling.

Hyman recalled one night so black that to figure out if it was safe to move he had had to crawl on his hands and knees. When his fingers hit a rough wood wall, Hyman grabbed one of its broken boards and pulled hard. The wall resisted his pressure. Confident that no night wind would blow it over, Hyman huddled against the wall for his usual vigilant sleep from which he could spring awake at the sound of a snapping twig.

No snap interrupted him. The sun crept over the horizon and lit the land and a country road thirty yards away. Hyman awoke, realizing that the wall he had slept against was the back of a barn whose front had buckled, tilting its moss-covered roof low so that it looked like an old stooped-shouldered woman bowing to pray.

It was the sixtieth straight morning Hyman had eluded marauders. When he looked at the field to his right, he could not believe his eyes. The tops of several large carrots and radishes bushed out of the soil. He walked carefully around the barn and looked into every window. It was just amazing; no one was sleeping inside.

He rushed into the field and dug up five carrots and seven radishes in a few minutes. Tired, seeing no predatory stragglers, he sat, his back resting against the barn. He saved the greens just in case he got desperate, put the roots in the other pocket, and started eating a carrot, his first food in two days.

The day had started out very lucky. As Hyman chewed the carrot slowly to protect his sore teeth and gums, he scanned the distance regularly. Halfway through his carrot, he spotted a head rising above a crest far down the road. He immediately ducked around the barn's side. When the person was in full view, Hyman saw that he was an emaciated man walking alone. When the man came closer and Hyman could distinguish his features, he was sure the man was Naftali Silverberg, the greengrocer from his hometown of Ravaruska. Naftali had not been close to the Schwartz family. But a year had passed since Hyman had seen anyone he had known before the war, let alone a *lantzman*. Seeing someone he knew still alive confirmed Hyman's most cherished belief. Excited, he ran toward the road, waving his arms and shouting, "Naftali. Naftali Silverberg."

The man looked at Hyman momentarily, and kept walking.

"Wait Naftali. I'm from Ravaruska."

The man stopped and watched Hyman brush past weeds and push aside bushes. When Hyman finally stood opposite him panting, the man looked him in the eye, said "Idiot" and walked on.

Hyman ran along the road after Naftali. In an act uncharacteristic of that cruel and selfish season, he offered Naftali a carrot. But the emaciated man refused it. "Idiot," he said and kept walking. Hyman ran in front of him. "Don't you recognize me, Naftali? I'm Hyman Schwartz, Abraham and Sara's son."

"Who you are doesn't matter. The question is, are you resting or stopping?"

"We're still alive, Naftali. What difference do words make?"

"All the difference in the world. When you're resting you're headed somewhere."

"Then I'm resting." Hyman saw that if Naftali did not eat

soon, he would die. In 1945, carrots were dearer than diamonds. Only a week earlier Hyman had seen a man take American dollars from a bank's bombed-open safe and use them as kindling for the fire he cooked an egg in. Money was paper. Food was life. Hyman wanted his *lantzman* to make it. He pressed a carrot into Naftali's hand. "Please," he said.

"Not for me," the ex-greengrocer answered.

"But you'll die if you don't eat."

"I'm not headed anywhere."

"With my own eyes I saw you going south."

"So this morning I'm headed south. Maybe tomorrow I'll go east." Naftali let the carrot drop and smiled sardonically. "Aren't you headed in the same direction?"

"I'm going back to Warsaw. That's where they took me from. I left Rava to go to university there."

"I know who you are, Hyman. It's where you're going that's got me confused."

"They took my wife and son from Warsaw. That's where they'll go back to. Shouldn't you go to Rava?"

"No one belongs in Rava."

Hyman figured Naftali was delirious from starvation. He picked up the carrot and held it to Naftali's mouth.

Naftali spit on it. "You were once a smart boy, Hyman. Did the university make your brains fall out?"

"I'm heading to Warsaw."

"And I'm heading to the moon. There's no Warsaw left."

"A city doesn't just disappear."

Naftali smiled a maniacal grin. "The boy's a lummox. He's seen that this new world makes anything possible and still believes that cities stand and Jews belong somewhere."

"You belong where you came from. I have a wife and son. I'm going to find them."

"Sure you are," Naftali cackled. "And I'm going to find the end of the rainbow. It's just over the next hill. No. No." Naftali scurried to the side of the road, fell to his knees and stared. "No. It's behind that rock. Not there?" Naftali got up, put a finger in his mouth and turned as if trying to select

66

a direction. "I'll just have to keep looking. I'll look for that pot of gold until I freeze to death." He threw his head back and laughed. "You're a lummox. The grave is where Jews belong."

"At least try." Hyman edged away. "You're still alive!"

"You call this alive?" Naftali slowly turned full circle, holding his ragged clothes away from his sides as if he were modeling a Paris designer's latest fashion. "The university took a smart boy and taught him to be a lummox. Tell me. Did your famous professors ever ask really important questions? Did they ever *try* to figure out why a man should go on when nothing's left?"

"There's always something. There has to be." Hyman rushed away northward. When he was ten yards away, he heard Naftali's maniacal cackles chasing after him. "You're not only a lummox, Hyman. You're also a *putz*, a first-class Yiddish *putz*."

Hyman was less than a day from Warsaw. Despite the extermination he had witnessed, he had to believe that Rachel and David had survived. And they would rush back to the apartment house. Hurry, he told himself. Hurry so they don't have to wait too long.

Hyman walked past shattered farmhouses, bomb-pocked fields, uprooted orchards, the shiny white skeletons of oxen and deer. Years of killing had swelled the vulture population; black shapes circled overhead continually. Naftali said Warsaw was gone. But Hyman knew that to save Notre Dame the French had surrendered Paris. Lining its streets, they had watched Hitler's troops goosestep down the Champs Élysées. Wouldn't Warsaw's cardinal do the same to guarantee that St. John's still glittered and that Sigismund's column stood proud?

Stragglers shook their heads and said that Warsaw was no more. But Hyman believed that something was left. Hope kept his feet walking and his fingers digging for edible roots.

When he finally reached Warsaw's outskirts late the next afternoon, he was incredulous. Churches had exploded;

buildings had disintegrated. Sides of tall buildings jutted from the Vistula's shallows. The bridge from Warsaw to Praga had collapsed; only the tops of its towers stuck out above the water's surface.

The closer Hyman came to Warsaw's center, the more complete the devastation was. Every tree was a stump. Steel girders stood naked, twisted rust monuments sprouting from rubble. Three-hundred-year-old buildings that had surrounded the city's medieval square, Stare Miasto, had collapsed into heaps of wood, brick and tile. Warsaw's most elegant street, the cobblestoned Faubourg de Cracovie, had been bombed so often that it was a cratered dirt path; the ornate Bristol Hotel was just one more rubble heap.

Warsaw had been a refined city, a grand city of palaces with porticoes and Doric columns. Six years of war had turned it aboriginal. Wherever a building stood, a family determined to guard its territory to the death had seized each room. But most people were not lucky enough to have indoor shelter. Heading toward the ghetto, Hyman watched roaming hoards claw through rubble searching for sugar cubes or a backyard garden's unharvested vegetables. Everywhere he looked, he saw people sifting through rubble, and vultures circling overhead, waiting to feed on the dead.

Halfway to the ghetto, he spotted a horde of bedraggled men carrying a large sheet made of rags sewn together. Since groups spelled danger for Jews, Hyman ducked behind a wall for protection. Each man held a rock that had been tied into the sheet's border with string and strips of leather. Hyman watched them inch stealthily toward a feeding vulture. Every time the vulture cocked its head back, the men froze as motionless as statues; the center of their sheet made a hollow flapping sound in the wind. When the vulture went back to tearing flesh off a corpse, the men inched closer.

What self-control they had! They took fifteen minutes to get within five feet. Their eyes were riveted on their tribal chief. He slowly raised his left hand, his fingers curled like a pistol. When his hand pointed directly overhead and his third finger pulled the "trigger," his warriors hurled the sheet directly over the vulture. The rocks in its borders pulled the parachuting sheet quickly down.

The bird flew frantically to the side. It thrashed under the cloth and raced to its edge. But the hunters had outwitted it. The tribal chief ran up and bashed in the vulture's skull. As a red stain expanded on the sheet, the horde hooted and shouted hallelujahs. Men slapped one another's backs as the sky started to darken. Hyman watched them, envying the fine evening those men would have. No matter how tough, musky, and sour vulture meat tastes, any fresh fowl is delicious when you're starving.

No one was exempt from labor. Cooking and tending the fires seemed to be women's jobs. Throughout the day children collected branches, took legs off broken furniture and pulled pieces of coal from the rubble. When their sacks were filled, the children dragged them, dropped the harvest in a pile beside their group's fire and went out for more. They worked until it became so dark that roaming became dangerous. Then everyone returned and huddled around the safety of the fire.

Hyman belonged to no group. It was late and the ghetto was still far away. Reluctantly, he decided to wait until the next morning to get there. That night he slept in a trench a hundred yards from the nearest fire. Wherever he looked he saw campfires with orange-red sparks rocketing into the night. Tomorrow I'll be home. Tomorrow Rachel, David and I will be together. After tomorrow no one will scare us again.

Dawn's first light woke him. He walked toward their apartment house as fast as his spindly legs would carry him. Hyman had heard rumors in Buna about a ghetto uprising a few months after he had been taken away. So he expected his apartment's windows to be blown out. Spring and summer were too far gone for crocuses, tulips, hyacinths and lilies to be forcing their way through the courtyard's soil like they had before the war. Another family, maybe several, would have taken over the apartment. But something would be left.

When Hyman saw what actually remained he stood for an hour staring. All that was left of his building were two front columns, smashed and jagged at their tops, and the two front steps that connected them. The walls, the gray cement flower boxes, the windowsills, the windows, mortar, bricks, fragments of shattered glass, broken furniture, drapes, dolls, cribs and roof tiles were heaped in a mound.

He finally collapsed on the top step, looking at the dirt path that once had been a paved street. When he was able to move again, he walked the path with his arm at his side as if Rachel would loop hers tenderly around it and would walk down the street beside him. Like a robot, he staggered along the rubble's side fifty times and turned what had been the corner as if turning that corner would make David materialize and come running toward him again, laughing, holding his arms wide open, shouting, "Papa. Papa. You're home." Hyman walked in a daze, unable to comprehend that after so many years of anticipating this moment, his son and the only woman he ever loved were not waiting.

In the half hour before sunset, he paced out the distance from the front steps to a point near the heap's northeast corner. He stumbled back over the rubble and paced the distance again, checking his orientation against the setting sun. When he reached the identical place a second time, toward a corner where the rubble was thin, Hyman was convinced he had found the spot. He knelt and burrowed, throwing aside bricks, mortar, tiles, wood, pieces of upholstery, and a doll's head. He scooped out earth, threw away parts of furniture and torn, dirt-encrusted remnants of an oriental rug. He discarded shards of glass, pieces of Jena saucers and Rosenthal china, until the light became so dim that he cut his hand digging.

He sat on the steps and watched a white crescent of moon rise, thin as a fingernail paring. His heart ached and his stomach turned as he peered into the distance. Hyman forced down a carrot and two radishes. He stood on the steps. "Lord, Our God, creator of suns and moons and the

universe itself, Your servant begs You to send Rachel back."
But night brought only one visitor: a drizzle that began
around eleven and fell until five the next morning.

When dawn broke, the scattered wet glass fragments
shone like millions of candles under the ascending sun. Hyman stared, hoping to see David and Rachel emerge from
the flames. But all he saw strewn to the horizon was a sea of
flickerings in which windowless walls and twisted girders
stood erect.

He dug in the rubble of the building's right-hand corner all
that second morning. For years, when everyone else in Buna
had asked, "Where is God?" Hyman had remained silent. He
believed that by not blaspheming the Lord, he would be
spared. As he threw aside mortar and glass, he knew that
when God sent back David and Rachel, or even just one of
them, Hyman Schwartz would consider the books balanced
and would ask no further questions. So he kept digging until
his fingers struck a right angle where wall met floor. He was
annoyed. Because his calculations had been slightly incor-
rect, he would have to spend extra time burrowing sideways
to the right. Be more careful, Hyman Schwartz. Checking
twice obviously isn't checking often enough.

After digging for another twenty-five minutes, Hyman's
fingers struck a large, upright piece of mortar. He pried it
loose; his fingertips felt the bricks with which he had surrounded the bundle. Pulling them out carefully, one by one,
he found the oilcloth-wrapped package, still whole inside.
Hyman unwrapped it. The manila envelope was not frayed.
Even its sharp edges were intact. He was amazed. His photographs had survived. He wanted to open the envelope, but
could not. Until Rachel and David were back, Hyman could
not bear to see their images.

He lifted a sliver of mortar and rubbed it between his
fingers like a worshipper with a holy talisman. Untying the
strings of the envelope with reverence, Hyman put the piece
of mortar behind the photographs, careful that it did not
scratch them. He retied the shoestrings, grateful that he

could carry away one concrete fragment of the place where he belonged. Pressing his forehead on the upper step, he prostrated himself and cried. "Please send them back. Please." But the cement did not reply. All that remained of his past was an envelope, two smashed columns and two cold stairs.

Hunger pains returned; Hyman foraged. Seeing a hopeful patch of grass a hundred yards from his house, he burrowed through it, tossing aside pebbles, gravel, and even a broken Kewpie doll. Just after one o'clock, he found and ate a small scrap of bread crust, and fifteen minutes later he found three fowl bones with some gristle left on them. He lapped water from a shallow puddle, confident that since the water had accumulated in last night's drizzle, cholera had not yet had time to spawn in it.

Around two thirty, Hyman saw a poster stapled to a stump. JEWISH RELIEF ORGANIZATION—BILDOWSKI AUDITORIUM. When he was a student living in a rented room, Hyman had walked past the Bildowski *Gymnasium* every day on his way to the university. So he knew exactly how to get there.

Miraculously, Bildowski had sustained only minor damage when the Germans systematically destroyed Warsaw after the Home Army uprising. Once there, Hyman waited, repeatedly asking the woman in charge of the line, "Is it time yet?" Finally, an official came out and directed him to a woman at a desk in the third of ten rows set up in the *Gymnasium*'s huge auditorium. Hyman rushed up to her and blurted out, "Please. I need to know. Do you have a record of Rachel and David Schwartz?"

The woman asked Hyman to please sit, and give her a moment.

But he leaned across the desk and implored, "Please, miss."

"Nancy Greenbaum is my name. Please tell me yours so I can help."

"Hyman Schwartz."

She wrote his name in capital letters on an index card, last name first. "Where were you and the people you are looking for born, Mr. Schwartz?"

Mister? Hyman thought. The last time someone called me "mister," he kicked me in the balls right afterward. "Please, miss. I'm from Ravaruska, but my Rachel is from—"

"The Ravaruska that's near Belz?"

"There is no other. But my Rachel was born in Cracow, David in Warsaw."

Miss Greenbaum stared at Hyman. "My grandfather came to Chicago from Ravaruska. But all the Greenbaums left Poland over sixty years ago."

Hyman had no interest in Miss Greenbaum's grandfather, nor in anyone else who had left an eon ago. "Please, miss. Please. My wife Rachel was born in Cracow and my son David in Warsaw."

Miss Greenbaum stood up. Hyman saw her clearly for the first time. Her cheeks were rosy. Her teeth were straight. She even smiled once in a while. Pearls hung down from her neck. She had breasts, not dried-out pouches, and they made soft curves in her new-looking sweater. As she threaded her way through the auditorium's pandemonium, twisting gracefully past other women, smiling apologetically when she jostled someone, steadily making her way to the library-style card files pressed against the far wall, Hyman squinted to follow her every move. She read the face of several cabinet drawers, slid one open, and pulled out two stacks of white cards. Winding her way back to Hyman, she flipped through a stack, turned one card upright, then flipped through the second.

"Sorry I took so long, Mr. Schwartz," she said and read the card she had marked. "Rachel Aronson Schwartz?"

"My wife is Rachel Lebenthal."

She went through the pack, and spoke gently. "There's nothing here. But this doesn't mean a thing, Mr. Schwartz. It's too early to know anything. Please take a seat. Can I get you some soup or . . ."

Hyman felt faint. The next thing he remembered was Miss

Greenbaum crouched beside him, waving a vial of smelling salts under his nose and calling, "Come quick, Sasha."

Vapors stung his nostrils. "My wife is Rachel Lebenthal. Where is she?"

"Please, Mr. Schwartz. We'll find her." Miss Greenbaum spoke to a heavyset woman with a red babushka tied around her head. "Sasha, don't let this man go."

Hyman tried to stand, but the heavyset woman held him in place, wiping sweat off his forehead with a handkerchief. "Mama," Hyman cried. He was sprawled between the desk and an aisle, his whole body shivering. "Mama, Mama, Wanda."

Miss Greenbaum came back quickly, holding a bowl of soup. A light vapor rose off its surface. She sat on the floor, cradled Hyman's head in the crook of her arm and spoon-fed him. "Eat slowly. I'm in no hurry."

Yellow circles of broth approached his mouth as if he were an infant. "Rachel," he said between mouthfuls. "My wife's maiden name was Rachel Lebenthal. Make Papa find her. I need my wife."

"Eat, Mr. Schwartz. You need food."

"I need Rachel." When the next spoon floated toward him, Hyman opened his mouth and ate. He did not ask about David. He was no fool. If Miss Greenbaum had found a card for David in the second stack, she would have said so, and would not have kept repeating, "I'm sure they will come back. New people turn up every day."

After finishing the soup, Hyman struggled to his knees. Dizzy and faint, he stayed on all fours for a moment.

"Give yourself time," Miss Greenbaum said. "Give me time to help you."

Hyman stood up on shaking legs, supporting himself on Miss Greenbaum's desk. "Rachel Lebenthal is my wife." He scanned the huge auditorium. All Hyman's life his father had pressured him to "make something" of himself. When Hyman left Rava to go to university, his father had encouraged him by saying, "Franz Joseph made sure that a new time has dawned for Jews. Study science and mathematics, Hyman. Don't ever become an old Jew, hiding in a corner, praying all day for the Messiah to come."

Hyman looked at the Bildowski ceiling and said bitterly, "Look at what I've become, Papa. Look at your new time for Jews."

Miss Greenbaum begged Hyman to sit so they could talk, but he tucked his manila envelope under his arm and headed out. She grabbed his other arm, but he pulled away. She shouted after him, "Please come back!"

But he left and stumbled back to his "apartment house." He sat on the top step, mourning. Rachel is my wife. When we married, I promised her my heart forever. Come back love, come back my beauty. He scratched his hand until his fingers drew blood the way glass had the night he dug for the envelope. Curling up on the top step, Hyman lay between the smashed, jagged columns, his body a wreath, the step his wife and son's cenotaph.

Miss Greenbaum's soup had staved off his hunger. As the sun set, Hyman stood up and screamed. "Take me too. Don't make me live for memories." He smashed a column with his fists; his friable skin tore; blood oozed from his knuckles. Pain helped him atone for being alive. Agony was his simplest obligation to all the ashes he had smelled drifting over Buna.

He stood and bayed at the sky. "Why didn't You take me too? Why should I live? Rachel and David were better than me any day in a million years."

He lay down but could not sleep. All night long he thought about them. When the next dawn finally came, Hyman waited on the top step, scanning the horizon, waiting for one of them to return. But around noon, with nowhere else to go, he returned to Miss Greenbaum.

She really seemed happy to see Hyman approaching her desk. She insisted that he sit down, and brought him soup again. When Hyman had finished it, he slumped back in the chair. "My Rachel? Please don't say she's dead."

"I wish I could give you a definite answer. An absolute yes or no would be much simpler, Mr. Schwartz. Maybe more painful, but clear-cut. It's this not knowing that can drive you nuts." She put her hand on top of Hyman's and held it warmly. "So far we have no report of them."

Hyman's face blanched.

"But just yesterday a worker located a woman's daughter in Copenhagen. Your wife and son could be in Hamburg or Moscow. I put their names on an international search."

"How long will it take?"

"Three, maybe four days from Cracow. Amsterdam and Scandinavia have been running around three weeks. And Moscow is in such bad shape, I can't predict how long they will take. But you have my word, Mr. Schwartz, no matter what we hear, the message will come to me and I'll figure out a way to contact you immediately." Miss Greenbaum's eyes settled on the gnarled twigs that were Hyman's fingers. "What sort of work did you do in the camp, Mr. Schwartz?"

"Whatever they told me to," Hyman said. "First, they put me in stupid work, but then for a while they used me in Buna, near Auschwitz. A big German company had a factory there. I helped develop mathematical models so they could figure out which synthetic rubber would make better replacement tires. Then they changed their minds and decided that intelligent work was the wrong way to use a Jew. So they sent me back to carrying rocks."

"Were you a mathematician?"

"What I was doesn't matter anymore. Now I do any work. Give me a shovel and I'll dig. Put a pick in my hands and I'll swing it. Show me rocks and I'll move them. Just find my family."

"If I knew what you did before the war, I might be able to find a position and a visa to go with it."

"I studied mathematics." Hyman did not betray his thoughts. Before the war is forever ago. Do you realize what I lost?

"That will help. It's easier to find a position for a man with a profession."

Miss Greenbaum also told Hyman that for the moment, not a single visa was available in all of Warsaw. "I'm sure you've already guessed how generous the world is to Jews, Mr. Schwartz. Countries all over the map say they only wish they weren't so busy feeding their own so they could take in a few more kikes! But getting a position will still be easier for a man with an education. And for a man from Ravaruska, I'll get a visa even if I have to forge one."

Hyman left Miss Greenbaum's desk knowing that no matter how sincere and sentimental she was, she would find a visa just about impossible to obtain. Wasn't it ironic? Because Hyman's father had pushed him to get a modern education, he had been saved from the ovens. The year he had spent in Buna gave him enough food and got him strong enough to survive the rest. But Papa never understood that it wasn't the university education that made a somebody from Hyman Schwartz. It was Rachel Lebenthal. And now he was nothing.

He began sleeping on the steps of the *Gymnasium* and was the first at Miss Greenbaum's desk every morning. Some days he came by again around lunchtime. When three weeks had passed, he kept up his hopes by banking on the "forever" Moscow could take. Rachel and David had to be alive.

One lunchtime in early November Miss Greenbaum gave him a piece of her Spam sandwich. "I'm what they call plump," she said. "Now that your stomach has had a few weeks' experience, you can digest a little meat. It will look a lot better on you than on me." She tried to sustain his spirits. But even though fall 1945 was unusually mild, by late October winds had whistled through the heaps of fallen bricks; nights of below-freezing weather had glazed Warsaw's devastation in white. Hyman wrapped his overcoat tightly around his frame, but the chill still leaked in as if through a strainer.

On the morning of November tenth, Miss Greenbaum was ecstatic. "Read this!" She extended a yellow telegram.

"All I understand is 'Rava.' I don't understand English."

"Well you're going to learn. The cable's from Dad." She translated it. " 'Visa coming for Rava, stop.' " She looked up. "Rava means you." She continued. " 'Two others, stop. Airletter follows, stop. Love, Dad.' " She grasped Hyman's shoulders. "Do you understand, Mr. Schwartz? You're going to America. I told you that you'd start a new life."

Hyman listened, but he could not feel the pleasure Miss Greenbaum did. He was still waiting.

A week later, Greenbaum's letter came from Chicago. For the mathematician from Rava, a friend of his had found a position with a New York accounting firm. He did not know the people personally, but he had been assured that the placement was solid.

"But I'm not an accountant," Hyman protested.

"Doesn't a mathematician need to be good with numbers? If you're good with numbers, you'll be great with accounts."

"What about Rachel?"

"I'll keep track of where you are. If I hear anything, good or bad, I'll wire you immediately."

Hyman knew far better than Miss Greenbaum that to a mathematician, an accountant was no better than an adding machine. As he sat beside her desk pondering, Hyman stepped over a mental threshold and re-entered a memory. He literally felt he was sitting in a large amphitheater at the university, listening to a lecture he had heard eight years earlier.

Professor Minkowski was young, tall, handsome and authoritative. "Mathematics is to accounting," Hyman remembered Minkowski booming, "what orchidology is to pig farming." Minkowski stood erect and pulled straight the handlebars of his mustache. His delicate gold watch chain fell flat against his vest front. He seized the lectern's sides, leaned aggressively forward, and pierced his audience with his razor blue gaze. "Mathematics is the pinnacle of human thought. A mathematician must be more than a philosopher. He never worries whether a *one* is an apple, a saw, or a feather. If a mathematician wishes, he can make each *one* nothing but his dreams. Which is why mathematics is to accounting what orchidology is to pig farming," Minkowski had said, and again leaned forward. "Because to the mathematician, the material object each *one* represents is irrelevant. But to the accountant, like to the Jew, every *one* is a shekel."

Maybe Miss Greenbaum was right. By Minkowski's standards, Hyman was perfectly suited to accounting. First, he was a Jew. More important, he preferred what Minkowski detested. If every *one* stood precisely for some unit of money, accounting suited Hyman just fine. Then no *one* could be a smashed and jagged column, a lost lover, or hope shattered. To have every *one* be just a shekel was salvation itself.

Miss Greenbaum was pleased that Hyman had come to his senses. She sent him to the American consulate's medical officer for a physical and to the Jewish Agency for papers.

After days of waiting, the Jewish Relief Organization found enough parts to put a rusted truck into good enough shape for the rough overland trip to Hamburg. On the evening before his departure, Hyman stumbled back to his apartment, knelt and kissed the top step. "I'll be waiting, Rachel. A boat will take me far away. But Miss Greenbaum promised she'll tell me the minute she finds you. I won't stop waiting. Please hurry. Without you I'm nothing."

Chapter Fourteen

HYMAN BOARDED the Panamanian freighter *Leviathan* in Hamburg. Although the crossing was smooth, he felt ill continuously. It was not the food, which was simple but substantial. And he knew he ought to appreciate receiving one of the precious few visas. Yet he felt oppressed and in mourning, as if he had abandoned his family for a strange place.

After ten days, the freighter pulled into New York Harbor. Hyman stood on the deck, staring at tall buildings that seemed to have sprouted from the river. A frigid breeze pricked his face. He held his blanket and envelope close to his side. They and the twenty dollars Miss Greenbaum had given him were all he really had. So he held them tightly, as if it were they, not he, who needed protection against icy air.

The old freighter creaked upriver past the Statue of Liberty. Passengers fore and aft, the huddled masses whose yearning she was there to encourage, grew excited. "Look at that," a man said, pointing to the thin outline of snow covering her. "The Sabbath Queen put on a wedding gown to greet us." Hyman looked on silently.

As they drew nearer shore, Hyman was surprised to see that a crowd of people was actually waiting as the *Leviathan* pulled up to the wharf. He had promised himself not to keep searching. But he could not resist the pull of those eager faces. He spotted a woman who looked like Rachel. His heart rose, tears filled his eyes. He started to shout to her. And oh my God! She was waving at him. Hyman started to wave back. She came closer to the ship. He stopped. The woman was not his wife.

Bundled up, fathers and sons, mothers and daughters, brothers, sisters, aunts, uncles and every other degree of relative were moving about and stamping their feet on the thin dusting of snow to keep warm in the frigid air. When a canvas-sided gangplank was rolled into place, a man in a blue uniform strode on board. Since all the refugees had received special clearance in Europe, the immigration officer had only to check each person's papers before letting him disembark.

Hyman watched people press forward. One woman ran down the gangplank; her bundles stretched its canvas sides. She fell to her knees and put her forehead against the slushy asphalt. A man pushed through the crowd and lifted her to her feet. When she saw the man's face, she screamed unintelligible words and hugged him frantically.

Hyman waited until the last. When all the other refugees had gone, he showed his papers to the immigration official and disembarked. He walked into pandemonium. On the wharf, relatives clutched, clasped, and bear-hugged one another, crying that by the time the telegram had arrived they had given up hope. Brother supported brother. Children cried "Momma, Momma." One nine-year-old girl wore a leopard coat and a hat that looked like a fighter pilot's. Her father swung her over his head, and sang. "Once she was my baby, look how big she's grown." Then he hugged her as if he would never let her go.

Hundreds who expected no one in particular paced the wharf simply because they had read in the *Jewish Daily Forward* that a boat was due. They waved placards: HAVE YOU SEEN MIREL GOLD? DO YOU KNOW THE WHEREABOUTS OF LEO SHULDER? One man grasped the coatsleeve of every disembarking passenger and implored, "Maybe you know my Shoshanah?"

Hyman walked hurriedly past the clusters of reunited and made his way to a Yiddish sign that said HEBREW IMMIGRANT AID SOCIETY. The woman who sat behind a desk near the sign worked busily. She wore tortoiseshell glasses and a heavy overcoat. While speaking to one immigrant at a time, she repeatedly had to ask people who had rushed to the front to wait. "Please," she said again and again. "I'm working as fast as I can. Please. I'll help each and every one of you. Please, please be patient with me."

Hyman went last. The woman, a Selma Aronowitz, listened to his story. She suggested he go to the Martinique Hotel, where HIAS had set up a facility with warm dormitories. She said that everyone there understood and would make every effort humanly possible to acclimate immigrants to the New World.

Hyman insisted he needed a room of his own, a place without other immigrants. He was waiting for his family, and had sworn to himself not to acclimate until they arrived.

She tried several tacks to convince him that the Martinique was the place to be. Finally, she realized that Hyman was adamant and pulled out a mimeographed list of names. She ran her fingers down it. When she stopped, she wrote a name on a blank piece of paper and drew a map on the other side. "The Excelsior Hotel," she said. "Here. Ask for Mr. Scheinberg. But first, please read this." She handed Hyman a long white envelope.

He opened it. It contained a crisp twenty-dollar bill and a note printed in English and translated into Dutch, Flemish, French, German, Greek, Hungarian, Polish, Russian, Serbo-Croatian, and Yiddish: "The Jewish Community of New York welcomes you. We hope and pray that this small gift will help you get started in your new life. If you are having difficulty, please call HIAS at LAckawanna 5-7171, any time, night or day. Our hearts go out to you. May our friendship be the companion you have missed these many years past."

Hyman took the map but handed back the twenty dollars. "Please, miss," he said in Yiddish. "I got one of these." Then he handed her the note. "Save them both for someone who needs them."

He crossed under the West Side Highway and stepped onto Thirty-second Street. He gaped at buildings, incredulous not simply because eight- and nine-story structures were numerous, but because their red brick sides were unpocked and their windows were intact. Understandably, the few trees lining New York City's side streets were bare this late in fall; but they actually still had branches. In Warsaw, only splintered stumps remained.

Hyman turned the corner of Thirty-second Street at Broadway. Strings of colored lights twinkling on and off were suspended from one side of the boulevard to the other. They were interspersed with large, shiny, colored bells, glittering foil stars, and lights in the shape of a long sleigh pulled by eight reindeer.

A sailor strode proudly past Hyman; a drunken woman hung from his arm. She staggered up to Hyman, her arms extended, and asked him a question in English. He shrugged his shoulders. She held out her arms, hummed, and turned in front of him several times. Hyman was perplexed; she seemed to want to dance. When he did not join, she looked at him crossly. Then she returned to her sailor and stumbled away laughing.

Hyman walked uptown. Poised mannequins modeled elegant clothes in display windows. A man in a real felt hat and a light-colored cashmere overcoat came out of a department store carrying in each hand a shopping bag brimming over with red boxes. Smiling mothers bought treats for their children: real chocolate bars at the newspaper stand, pretzels from the stack on a vendor's dowel, and frankfurters from a steaming cart. What a place, Hyman thought. Three weeks earlier, he had left Warsaw, a city stripped of dreams, a city of cratered streets and aboriginal hordes.

He hurried uptown. At Fifty-eighth Street, he saw the Excelsior Hotel and walked into its aging lobby. He touched the counter hesitantly as if it were a mirage that might swirl and dissipate. But the wood was real and the silver desk bell rang when he depressed its nipple. The bell even brought forth a man to the counter. He was moon-faced and impish; wisps of white hair flew from his temples. Smiles creased the corners of his eyes.

By contrast, Hyman was a ghost: pale, scrawny, unshaven, and wearing an overcoat three sizes too big for his body.

"You look tired, mister," the man said. Hyman was silent. "You don't speak English, is that it? *Rets di Yiddish?*" When Hyman nodded yes, the man went on in Yiddish, *mama lushen*, the mother tongue. "From all over the world people send friends here. So who sent you?"

"Miss Aronowitz," Hyman said. "From HIAS."

"From HIAS!" Months ago, Moishe Scheinberg had promised his linen supplier that if HIAS needed a room for a refugee, he would provide one on credit, no questions asked. The war ended, refugees landed, but no one had come to the Excelsior. Scheinberg had been sad to conclude no one ever would. "That was so smart of her. You need a room, right?"

Hyman nodded.

"Are you in luck! Even though I'm expecting a very big group any day now, a veritable convention mind you, I have a room that's going to make you as happy as if you'd just won ten straight games of pinochle." Scheinberg took a key off the wooden rack under the counter. "Number four thirteen. With a view of Broadway, no less." He walked to the stairs jauntily, motioned for Hyman to follow, and gabbed as they ascended. "You hear a number like four thirteen and you think, 'There must be twenty, maybe thirty rooms on every floor.' Well I'm sure a smart man like you appreciates the intimacy of a small place. But America thinks big and good are the same thing. So a few years ago I said to myself, 'Moishe. Don't be an idiot. Put three numbers on every room so when someone from far away writes, they'll be impressed and will think, "That fellow must have some big place." ' " Scheinberg tapped the thicket of white flying around his right temple. "Smart. No?"

They reached the second floor. Hyman said nothing. Scheinberg kept ascending. "My cousin Alfred isn't much of a talker either." On the third-floor landing, he stopped and turned to Hyman. "Do you feel all right?"

Hyman looked up at Scheinberg and nodded.

"Maybe you should see a doctor? I mean you should get a real specialist to examine you. I'm sure I can get you an appointment with one of the best, a doctor's doctor. He even teaches at Mount Sinai one day a week." Mr. Scheinberg scratched his head. "If I knew your name that is."

"Hyman Schwartz." He became pensive remembering the doctors at the DP camp in Hamburg tapping on his chest and drawing his blood for their tests. "I've already been checked over, Mr. Scheinberg."

"And what did they tell you?"

"That if I eat enough, I'll become like I was before the war."

"Then you're in luck. America has enough food to feed this world and two others." Scheinberg patted his potbelly. "Look at me. Jews shouldn't eat pigs. So they shouldn't eat like pigs either. But if a man eats like a canary, what's the use of being alive?" He started up the next flight of stairs. "And food here isn't expensive like in Europe. Here, on a working man's wages you can eat a toasted bialy or a bagel with every breakfast. Schmaltz herring you can have as often as you like. How does that sound, Mr. Schwartz?"

Hyman shrugged. When everyone else had gone hungry during the Depression, the well-off Schwartz family always had more than enough food. But then came the ghetto, and Buna after that. Times had changed again. In the past week Hyman had eaten three bowls of oatmeal a day. He did not yearn for bialys or herring. He yearned only for a cable from Nancy Greenbaum. He needed the cable the same desperate way the starving need food

"Since it's food you need, Mr. Schwartz, in a few weeks you'll feel like new." Scheinberg stopped on the fourth-floor landing to catch his breath. "A talker I can see you're not.

Me? All my life I've been a big mouth." Scheinberg turned right and led Hyman down the narrow, dimly lit hall. "When you get food in your stomach, you'll feel settled in. I'll bring you a sandwich."

Hyman shook his head. "I can take care of myself."

"Of course you can. But you must have had a plenty hard day, and Moishe Scheinberg won't take no for an answer." Scheinberg stopped and faced Hyman. "Do you keep kosher?"

Hyman shook his head no.

"Then tomorrow I'll send you to Horn and Hardart's. They sell sandwiches in the Automat section and hot meals in their cafeteria. For only a little more you can drink all the coffee you want. You might also be interested in the Hebraishe Club. I go there every Wednesday night for pinochle. Do you play pinochle, Mr. Schwartz?"

Hyman shook his head no.

"Look. I know life's been more than hard for you fellas. But it's time to start again. Learning pinochle would take your mind off what you've been through." Leaning toward Hyman, he lowered his voice. "I know a little about that too, Mr. Schwartz. The club has a minyan every morning and night."

"A minyan?" Hyman said.

"You're entitled to nine men to say amen to your Kaddish."

Hyman stared into Scheinberg's eyes and said nothing.

"I came to New York in 1922 and I have plenty of Kaddishes to say. It's the only way to feel a little better. Go to the club. Say Kaddish. You have to say good-bye somehow." When Hyman remained silent, Mr. Scheinberg rubbed his hands together as if they needed warming. "To each his own." He walked on down the hallway's narrow carpet runner. "A friend of mine said that Jews in America should stop saying Kaddish altogether. Here no one sings the 'Volga Boatman.' In America everyone likes 'On the Sunny Side of the Street.' You couldn't know that song yet, Mr. Schwartz. Maybe after a while in America you'll be smiling and whistling it too. Just you wait and see."

Scheinberg stopped near the end of the hall, unlocked the

room, and threw the door wide open. "Now you tell me, Mr. Schwartz. Is four thirteen the room of your dreams?"

To Hyman it was. The twin-size bed had both mattress and boxsprings, rather than four tiers of planks for twenty skeletons to crowd up on. The table beside the bed was sturdy, if slightly chipped, with rosette patterns carved into its wooden borders. The table lamp had a tall opalescent base with a likeness of an amusement park parachute jump painted on it. A green carpet covered the floor; a solid chest of drawers was flush against the far wall. The room had its own white sink, its own closet, and in front of the window, its own maroon velvet wing chair.

"And that's not all," Scheinberg said. He slid the wing chair aside, and pressed his left cheek up to the window-pane. "Look out there, Mr. Schwartz."

Hyman did not move.

"No need to worry. My hotel is built from bricks, girders and the strongest glass. Listen." He tapped the glass with his knuckles. "Solid." He pointed right. "If you lean close and look over there you'll see Broadway."

Hyman stayed away, looking directly out the window in-stead. Against the darkening sky, he noticed the outlines of water tanks and metal ladders topping the roofs across Fifty-eighth Street. But what really caught his eye was a painted advertisement on the building's side: on its left side, the billboard portrayed a headless side of beef, neck down, lower legs cut off as though hanging in a butcher shop. On its right side was printed ABELMAN'S MEATS. SINCE 1905.

Scheinberg walked over to Hyman. "Anything you want to know about this neighborhood, just ask Moishe Schein-berg. And for you, all this is only fourteen dollars a week. But please don't tell anyone how little I'm charging you." Scheinberg saw Hyman weighing the price. "Now if four-teen dollars is too much, under these very special circum-stances I can negotiate."

Hyman handed the twenty-dollar bill, all the money he had, to Scheinberg.

"Are you crazy? You've got to eat. You've got to get a haircut and shave. You'll pay me when you land a job."

Hyman pulled out the paper Miss Greenbaum had given him. "I don't need charity. I have a job. It's at 1225 Broadway."

"How many months passed between when they gave you that job and now?"

"It's just a few weeks. Miss Greenbaum said everything was arranged."

"And I'm sure she meant it. But what they say there and what happens here aren't always identical."

"But she said I'd be an accountant."

Scheinberg breathed easy. "Oh! Why didn't you say so? There's always work for an accountant."

"But I'm not an accountant."

"You just said—"

"That's what Miss Greenbaum made me say." Hyman scratched his hand nervously. "I told her ten times that I'm not an accountant. But she kept saying not to worry. What should I do? I'm not an accountant. I better go there right now."

"Now they're locking up. After a night's sleep, a shower, a real breakfast and a trip to the barber, you'll go to that firm of yours. Trust Moishe Scheinberg. That firm's going to hire you no questions asked."

Hyman had no more fight left in him. He heard the door shut behind Scheinberg and reluctantly sat in the chair. He scratched his hand nervously.

Five minutes later, Scheinberg returned with a cheese sandwich and a steaming glass of honeyed tea. He put them on the windowsill. "Eat. Sleep. I put fresh towels in the closet, and drew a map to get you to 1225 Broadway. Sleep well, Mr. Schwartz. I know it was awful. But the bad times are over. Tomorrow you'll get that job no questions asked."

After Scheinberg left and Hyman was finally alone, he faced the door and spoke as if the hotel man were still there. "Please don't look at me with sad eyes and tell me you know how awful it was. If you weren't there, you can't imagine. So please don't look at me like you understand. Look at me like you never could."

Hyman suddenly realized he might not be alone. Certain that demons and dybbuks haunted his room, he crouched, put the lamp on the floor, and looked under the bed. Although he saw no ghosts, experience had taught him never to trust appearances. He ran his fingers under the bedframe, and scoured the wainscoting, moldings, ceiling, and corners of the room. Nothing. He investigated further. The sink was dry, the towels clean, the hangers empty, and the high shelf bare. Hyman locked the door, put the lamp back on the table and sat down. Exhausted, he ate the sandwich slowly, sipped the honeyed tea, and finally fell into his usual dreamless sleep, from which he could awaken at the snap of a twig.

Chapter Fifteen

THE NEXT MORNING Hyman took a quick shower, had a haircut and shave and raced to 1225 Broadway. He found Teitlebaum & Sharfenstein, Accountants, on the index of tenants, and bounded up two flights of stairs. Nervously entering the waiting room, he showed the receptionist the note from Miss Greenbaum. The woman made a call and a well-dressed man came out.

When Hyman first laid eyes on that man, he was sure he had landed on another planet. The man's jacket was Harris tweed, solid-gold links closed his shirt cuffs, which were not frayed, and his regimental tie was silk. His eyes were bright, his smile was broad, and his teeth were straight and unbroken.

"In Warsaw Miss Greenbaum said I should talk to Mr. Teitlebaum," he said in Yiddish, and showed the man the note.

The man's voice surprised him. In contrast to his attire, his voice was earthy and Galician. "If you're from Warsaw, you've come to the right place. I'm Sam Teitlebaum, and you are . . ."

"Hyman Schwartz."

"Let's go to my office so we can talk in private."

Hyman looked at the huge room, at men working, at secretaries typing. He was sure that no war had touched these extraterrestrial beings. In the boss's office, Teitlebaum asked Hyman whether he wanted coffee, tea, perhaps a schnapps. Hyman said that he was neither thirsty nor hungry; Teitlebaum started searching through a pile of documents on his desk.

"I'm not too late?" Hyman asked anxiously.

Sam Teitlebaum kept looking, as if hunting for the right document. "Jack Rossberg usually sends the papers over in advance." He looked through a few more documents. "The note says that you're an accountant."

"No! Please believe me. I told Miss Greenbaum that I never studied accounting, but she insisted that . . ." Hyman's voice trailed off. No explanation could change facts: Hyman Schwartz was not an accountant. Despondent, he got up and started toward the door.

"Calm down, Mr. Schwartz," the boss said. "You've got a job."

Hyman knew he was hallucinating and kept walking. But Teitlebaum came after him, put a soft hand on his shoulder and said, "You're hired."

Hyman stood in place, immobile and incredulous.

Teitlebaum turned Hyman around and looked him in the face. "You're hired, Mr. Schwartz. That's all there is to it."

As the words sank in and Hyman realized that this boss had taken pity on him, he became animated. "You won't regret hiring me, Mr. Teitlebaum. I'll work double hard to learn accounting. Just give me a chance. I'll stay late every night. I'll study in my room. I'll do whatever you ask. You have my word."

"I'm not a slavedriver, Mr. Schwartz. You'll decide how hard you need to work. You have three months to learn basic bookkeeping. Learn it and you get more time to learn accounting. Although I'm sure you will catch on, if you can't, I'll locate a more suitable job. Have I made myself clear?"

Hyman nodded. Three months was three months longer than he had anticipated. "Can I start right away?"

"You'll start soon enough, Mr. Schwartz." Sam massaged

his temples with his fingertips. "I hope you won't take offense. Perhaps you'll appreciate what I'm about to say since I see you already went through the trouble of getting your hair cut. You don't speak English. If a policeman stops you, you won't be able to explain that you have a job."

"Why should a policeman stop me? Miss Greenbaum said that in America no one bothers Jews."

"That's right. And Jewish vagrants end up in the same jails as gentile vagrants. That's democracy."

"I'll work hard. You won't need to call the police."

"It's just an expression, Mr. Schwartz. I would never call the police on you. This is America, not Germany. You have three full months to prove yourself," Sam said. "All I'm suggesting is that you buy new clothes. I'll advance you the money and every week I'll deduct ten dollars from your pay to get it back. By the end of three months, I will have deducted enough to pay for your clothes."

In three months? When an ordinary man worked in Ravaruska, he saved for three months just to buy a pair of boots. Three months. "I'll do whatever you want, Mr. Teitlebaum. But shouldn't you at least wait to see what work I can do before you advance me money? Maybe I won't be able to learn."

"Please, Mr. Schwartz. You have three months." Sam put on his overcoat and rubbed the sleeve. "Pure camel's hair, Mr. Schwartz. One hundred dollars at Sak's. Thirty-five at Mr. Feldman's. Let's go."

The rest of the afternoon swirled by like a kaleidoscope. Sam drove downtown in his Buick. For Hyman, everything was disconnected images: dashboard, traffic signals, tall buildings, cramped shops, pushcarts, buy an apple, vendors, crowds, people, pushing, yelling, bargaining, knishes, Chinese restaurants, Italian sausages. Sam showed Hyman a tenement with garbage heaped against its stained walls. "America's been good to this Jew," he said. "That's where I was born. But don't be misled. The place has been modernized and rebuilt since my day."

Hyman saw Italians, Poles, Chinamen, and Negroes. But the shocking fact was that at all the shops Sam took him to, people spoke Yiddish. Hyman could not believe that so many Jews were left. Since Hyman had said that any clothes would do, Sam did the selecting: a brown suit and dark overcoat, a hat so dark brown that it was almost black, three shirts, underwear, socks, shoes, an understated paisley tie, and a black leather belt. When Sam selected the suit, Hyman had to get up on a short wooden stool so the tailor (who said, "So you're a friend of Sam the Man") could mark the needed alterations with white soap. And the tailor was experienced enough to leave extra space for Hyman to grow into.

In two hours Sam had bought Hyman an entire wardrobe and was driving to the Excelsior. As they rode, Hyman looked, no marvel left in him. He stared at huge bridges filled with cars and passenger trains. When Sam rounded Manhattan's southern end and headed uptown on the West Side Highway, Hyman watched the city of factories and warehouses lining the highway's right side. Then he glanced to the left at the string of wharves flashing by. Speeding past Thirty-second Street in a sea of cars, he looked through Sam's window and caught a glimpse of the *Leviathan* tied up at its wharf. Following it as it receded through the back window, Hyman was pensive. Only yesterday he had left that wharf, scared and uncertain. And now, he was speeding away in a fancy automobile. Just as Miss Greenbaum had said, in America a man can become anything. In less than twenty-four hours, Hyman Schwartz had found a room and secured a job. Maybe Miss Greenbaum's cable would arrive tomorrow.

"We start work at eight in the morning," Sam said. "For the next few days, come to work dressed as you are. I'll be on the Lower East Side Sunday and will pick up your clothes. After Monday I'll expect you to wear them." Sam paused for a moment. "I hope you forgive my forcing you to wear new clothes even if you don't want to."

Hyman said nothing. No man on probation can tell a boss that he would wear mourner's clothes for all the family he had lost and whose ashes he had smelled in Buna's air. He would take them off only when Rachel and David returned.

"I wouldn't answer either, Mr. Schwartz. Personally, I don't care how you dress. But you don't speak English, and frankly, new clothes will help keep peace with my partner. He wants no immigrants at the firm. I hope you understand. If I owned the firm all by myself, I wouldn't give a damn how you dressed."

The next morning, Hyman was at the office early. When Sam arrived, he told Hyman that Himmelstein, one of the accountants, would teach Hyman basic bookkeeping principles.

"Give me one set of ledger sheets," Hyman said. "Give me a chance to figure the basics out myself. Then I'll be able to ask intelligent questions."

Sam gave Hyman worksheets and a recently vacated cubicle. When he heard from Hyman again late Friday afternoon, Sam marveled at how much Hyman had figured out in just two days. Hyman asked where numbers on the worksheets came from; Sam said they were copied off of invoices.

"Maybe you could lend me a worksheet and its invoices over the weekend?"

Sam gave him one from the dead file. Hyman studied all weekend. By the time he changed into his new clothes on Monday, oversize as they were, he had mastered entering and checking invoices. He was relieved: a mathematician could at least be a bookkeeper. But Sam said that even for bookkeeping, he needed more, either handwritten calculations or adding-machine tapes.

"Why? My head does perfect work faster."

"In accounting, heads aren't good enough. Clients need records. So do auditors."

So for the next week and throughout the next weekend, Hyman practiced on the adding machine. It was obviously based on the principle of the abacus. Hyman realized that the trick was mastering its rhythm. By his third week at the firm, he was adequate, if not yet proficient, with it.

Whenever Sam came by to check on him, Hyman tried to be subtle when asking whether a cable had arrived. When Sam asked what Hyman was waiting for, Hyman would answer, "Some news. Just some news." Each time Sam said that no cable had come, Hyman became despondent and compulsively scratched his hand.

It took Sam a month to realize that Hyman's talents were unique. Then he lavished praise on Hyman. But Hyman was indifferent to the fact that his talents were spectacular and that the speed with which he grasped principles was arresting. A month after that, Sam told Hyman his progress was so remarkable that the probationary period was to end a month early and that he would be retained with a raise. Hyman thanked Sam but said that he did not need more money and returned to his books.

In subsequent years, Hyman made only two requests. In 1947, he asked for a cubicle farther to the office's rear; in 1950, he requested the recently vacated cubicle beside the emergency exit. Once ensconced there, Hyman grew more withdrawn with each passing year.

Although he became more and more odd as a man, he became remarkable as an accountant. In ten years with the firm, Hyman had never made an arithmetical mistake. He devised unique systems of depreciating equipment, and invented what became an industry standard for calculating the exact amount of cloth needed to make any size garment, which allowed companies to charge the government on a more accurate cost-plus basis. Furthermore, he never missed a single day's work, never took one day's vacation, never complained, and never asked for a raise. He arrived promptly at eight every morning, earlier whenever necessary. Although he was on salary, during tax season he often worked well past midnight and would not accept overtime. "It's my job," he said.

After Sam Teitlebaum and Timothy Sharp (formerly Adolf Sharfenstein) dissolved their partnership late in 1946, Hyman kept Sam to his word. He wore the first suit Sam bought him until the seat of its pants was polished to a shine and its seams had been torn and resewn countless times. After ten years, his overcoat came to look like a patchwork quilt. And even on hot, humid days, Hyman closed his increasingly frayed shirt up to its top button and never loosened his pilled paisley tie. By 1948, Hyman spoke English and looked like a vagrant. Sam never said a word about it. Nor did Hyman.

By becoming the best accountant at the firm, Hyman had dramatically exceeded what he had promised and Sam felt obliged to stick to his word that without a partner, Sam wouldn't care how Hyman dressed. Although reason told Hyman that he was being irrational, he continued to believe tenaciously that Miss Greenbaum's cable—RACHEL IS IN MOSCOW—actually might arrive someday. David had been so young when he was rounded up; perhaps he didn't remember his original name. But he could return. He had to.

So when Hyman first spied Shimshon slouched against his doorjamb, he was looking for David. And by Thanksgiving 1955, Hyman had begun to teach Shimshon as if he were a son.

Chapter Sixteen

HYMAN SPENT most of Thanksgiving day engrossed in memories. But when he left his room Thursday afternoon and walked down Broadway, and when he strolled through Central Park on Saturday morning, he found himself looking at faces hoping to see Shimshon. And each time he returned to his room, he leaned his forehead on the window and studied every passing male face on the street below, wishing that even from four floors up he would recognize Shimshon. One night he actually dreamt that a young redheaded boy knocked on his door at the Excelsior, but would not enter the room because the sink was urine-stained. Was the boy in the dream David or Shimshon? Hyman awoke sweat-soaked and chastised himself for even imagining that David might have come back. He hated the effect Shimshon was having on him. You're an idiot, simply an idiot to believe Mr. Just Shimshon is even a bit like your son.

The Thanksgiving holiday's four days seemed interminable. Hyman awoke almost happy when Monday finally arrived. He put on the cleaned clothes he had picked up on Saturday morning and rushed to Fliegel and Pulka's.

As he crossed Broadway, he found himself humming a Yiddish tune his father had taught him, "*Shein vi di livana*" ("She Is as Beautiful as the Moon"). Arriving at 1225 precisely at eight, he was excited. In just four hours he would be teaching Shimshon. Anticipating the happy noon, he said "Good morning" as he took his work off Faye's desk.

"And good morning to you, Mr. Schwartz," Faye answered, sounding pleased at Hyman's uncharacteristic show of attention.

Hyman muttered a few unintelligible words and hurried away, disturbed because Faye had smiled at him the way a woman smiles at a man she likes. Putting her out of mind, he worked until eleven thirty, when thoughts began to distract him again. What had Shimshon's Thanksgiving been like? Did he sit around telling the boss's family how good he had had it before the war? Maybe he never had it so good? Maybe before the war everything was so terrible for him that when he eats Mrs. Teitlebaum's turkey, the good tastes are brand-new and he tells himself that because for twenty-five years he had it bad, for the next twenty-five he's guaranteed to have it good. I've never met Mrs. Teitlebaum, Hyman thought. But I once saw her at the office. She's pretty, like Mrs. Sondheimer. Hyman recalled Faye's smile and chased it away. A woman's smile is for young men. A woman lets boys dream, but I know what having a woman really means. And I know how it feels to lose her. No one else will be my wife. And Shimshon's not my son. I'll teach him for his father's sake.

Let him learn, let him leave. The truth is that it wouldn't bother me one bit if I never saw him again. That's right. I have to push him and be rough on him so he'll learn well. In fact, throwing out students who've finished learning is a teacher's job. A student who once tastes good teaching never wants to leave. A teacher has to order him: "Sonny! It's time for you to learn from the world. Go to Zion or to wherever you want." Mark my word, Hyman Schwartz. The day will come when you'll have to throw that young man out.

By noon, Hyman again had persuaded himself that he was in control; he didn't really care about Shimshon. Eventually, he would throw him out. So when Shimshon appeared, Hyman simply ate quickly and silently. As soon as they had finished lunch, he spread out Shimshon's worksheet and hunched studiously over it. His index finger slid down the paper line by line. In the middle of the page he closed his eyes for a moment, checked a calculation in his head, said "That's right," and continued moving down the page. Seven numbers from the bottom, his finger halted again. "Mistakes." He shook his head. "Like I told you, mistakes are the accountant's cancer. And almost every one is simple." Hyman pointed. "Look at that."

"At what?"

"At that!" Hyman underlined the spot in pencil. "How many mistakes did we find last week? That's another one. I learned a lot of arithmetics, but never one where nine plus four makes twelve."

Shimshon shook his head and chuckled. "I can't believe I did that."

"Believe it. And believe me you're not the first who can't do good accounting because he can't do passable bookkeeping. Laugh at that mistake, but it's an unexploded bomb. If you're lucky, it won't go off. If you're not you'll lose an arm."

"One mistake isn't a tragedy."

"Every mistake is a tragedy. For some you don't end up paying. But I know men who spend their whole lives crying because of one simple mistake."

"I'll fix it and be more careful."

"What if your next worksheet is one that only Abromowitz supervises? Would you know a mistake was there?" Hyman leaned toward Shimshon. "Breathe your work. Smell it. Know it so well that any mistake disgusts you like you'd just smelled shit."

"I said I would be more careful."

"I know what you said. It's what you'll do that worries me." Hyman stared at Shimshon. "What happens if you lose so much money that the boss says there is no next worksheet?"

"Sam would never fire me for one mistake."

"This isn't the Jewish Agency. It's a business and a business is here to make money. So don't depend on the boss's generosity, about which I'm sure he's lectured you a hundred times. Let him depend on you."

"Sam's been a prince to me."

"Every man is a prince when you make him money. You're better off when the man you work for needs you a lot more than you need him." Hyman folded his hands. "There's no way you could understand accounting right away, but if you want to learn what I can teach, you have to spend a lot more time practicing."

"I work plenty hard already."

"Yeah? How often do you work until ten at night? And when was the last time you stayed until the next morning? Never?" Hyman nodded. "Right?"

Shimshon nodded back.

"Thank you for being honest. Did you ever wonder why all the older men work late? Maybe you think it's because they don't have a good woman at home. You don't remember twenty years ago when men shuffled from one door to the next begging for work. Any work. Soon it will be tax season. Then you'll see how much work a man has to put in after he's mastered basic techniques, just to be your average, competent accountant. And those techniques, sonny, you haven't even begun to master."

"I'm working hard. Even Sam says my work is pretty good."

"If all you want is 'pretty good,' learn from Abromowitz. You know what I see when I review your work? Sloppy pages filled with simple mistakes all made for the same reason—because you're in a hurry. Do you really think that running fast now will make up for time you lost?"

"What do you want me to do?"

"I want you to start thinking about where you're headed. If you run through your worksheets now, you'll race through your ledgers later. Not because you'll be so fast. Later you'll run like a chicken without a head, never sure where you went wrong. And during your second week of searching, nice Mr. Teitlebaum will stop by your cubicle every five minutes just to ask, you know, 'Did you find that mistake yet? Do the books balance?' After two days of visits, you'll wish you had practiced my lessons. And after four weeks of reviewing line after line, worksheet after worksheet, the truth will finally dawn on you: You can't just go back to old work. You have to start all over. So if you want your old work to be finished once and for all, take your time. Take your time."

"I'll take my time. I'll take my time." Shimshon picked up his worksheet and left Hyman's cubicle, muttering "Asshole" all the way to his own cubicle, unsure how much longer he would be able to tolerate that niggling prick. But as evening approached, he heard machines in all the other cubicles still adding and realized that Hyman had told him the truth. Shimshon worried that back in Hungary he had adopted some work habits that the Economic Ministry had considered acceptable.

Until going to the Ministry after finishing technical school, Shimshon had settled for nothing but the best. He had been an apprentice twice before coming to New York. When he was just a young boy, he had worked after school and on weekends in the family's prosperous tailor shop. He had stuck close to his father, who was engrossed in the business and taught every detail to Shimshon.

His father had taught him how to rub a fabric between your fingers to see if the weave was high-quality, and how to check the seams your workers made to be sure they would last for years. He had even taught Shimshon the art of charming good customers and of serving them well, particularly the military officers and aristocrats, who had the finest clothes made for them and whose patronage assured that a Budapest business prospered. What Shimshon had detested in the government's Economic Ministry was the sloppy techniques the accountants used and the poor teaching apprentices got.

Now that he had a terrific accounting teacher, Shimshon

wanted to keep him. So for the first time since coming to New York he stayed late into the evening, recalculating worksheets and ledgers. At the next lunch, Hyman noticed the difference. "Now these I call worksheets."

Shimshon started to stay late every night, practicing the bookkeeping techniques Hyman taught him. Hyman's lessons were of several varieties. Some focused on using machinery accurately. Others concentrated on mastering techniques that promised to speed an accountant's work indirectly, because they improved his accuracy and thereby diminished (Hyman said "eliminated") the prospect of unfavorable audits. But the central thesis of both mechanics and techniques was moving slowly, focusing on details, reducing every procedure to its most minute components. And overarching all Hyman's lessons was one single art, Hyman's religion, what he called "meticulousness."

On Wednesday, Hyman focused on working with an adding machine. "You have to make Victor part of yourself. Only when he's an extension of your fingers will you really work fast with him. Match your timing to his. If you don't, you'll pull the handle too soon and he'll jam. Or his paper will get stuck or his keys won't depress. When any of those things happens, you're missing the rhythm. To really work *with* Victor you have to become one with his pace." Hyman sat in front of the machine, operating it. First he went slowly. Then he speeded up the rate at which he entered numbers. When he was moving at top speed, his fingers waltzed on the buttons. "Do you hear the rhythm?"

Frustrated, Shimshon shook his head.

Hyman stopped calculating and drummed the beat on his desktop. "Did you hear it that time?"

"Maybe. Let me try."

Shimshon took the swivel chair and imitated Hyman. But he jammed Victor. Hyman again drummed the rhythm on the desktop. Shimshon tried, but he jammed the machine again.

"Like I told you," Hyman said. "Victor takes practice.

Practice and patience. Follow his lead. Listen to him. If you push him the wrong way he'll click very loud and won't budge. Treat him gently and he'll obey your every command."

Shimshon tried several more times but kept jamming the machine. "Damn. How do you go so fast?"

Hyman pushed his hands to the bottom of his pants pockets. A flicker of a smile crossed his face. "By first having learned to go slow."

Chapter Seventeen

HYMAN WALKED TO WORK on Tuesday, December 20. The day was cold and dreary; from a low mist, snowflakes materialized, drifted down and adhered to coats and sidewalks. Although Faye was not at her desk when Hyman got upstairs, he assumed that she had arrived already, since his work was off to one side of her desk and two fresh coffee cakes were in its center. He set aside thoughts of the day, the month and the season and worked unabated until the ten-thirty coffee break. Loud voices in the corridor mentioned today's party to celebrate Hanukkah's first day. "Miracle of miracles, Shimshon," he heard Abromowitz say. "My wife baked me a honeycake for the party."

Pausing for a moment, Hyman detected the faint aroma of coffee and the scent of sweet cakes. They brought to mind his parents' home. If the conference room looked anything like his parents' Hanukkah celebrations, it would be jammed with people talking fast, laughing, drinking schnapps and reaching toward a table overflowing with food to take a slice of honeycake or a piece of schmaltz herring.

Hyman went back to work until just before eleven, when voices in the corridor interrupted him again. Then they silenced. Typewriters started typing, adding machines began adding and the office returned to normal. Hyman resumed work.

At noon Shimshon strode in and filled the desk with Gristede's food. "That Hanukkah table had a dozen honeycakes, *tzweibachs* and *boimikuchens*. Faye brought a delicious coffee cake. She asked me why you didn't come to try it."

"I have much too much work."

"We all have too much work."

"But some of us do it."

"And others make a little time for something other than balances." Shimshon lifted his chicken sandwich and toasted Hyman with it. "To your health, Mr. Schwartz."

"I'm surprised you still have room."

"I always have room for this," he said, taking a bite of the juicy sandwich. "And for this," he said, biting into the pickle. "This pickle is like your lessons. Sometimes sour but always the best. No matter what I eat in the conference room, I'd never pass up a lunch with you."

"This week."

"Cut it out. I may have had one schnapps too many, but I don't lie. I'm sticking with you. Let me tell you, that conference room was wild. This party was worth waiting for! Everybody was a little tipsy. After I finished my fourth slice of cake, Himmelstein came up to me. 'My wife makes the world's best apple strudel,' he said and winked. 'Try a piece.' So I did. He put his arm around my shoulder. 'No matter how bitter life gets, a wife's apple strudel still tastes sweet. You know, Shimshon,' he whispered, 'I know a girl, from a fine family mind you, who by a fluke of fate just happens to be available right now.' I chuckled, which got Himmelstein angry. 'Why are you laughing at my daughter?' he said. I apologized and told him that I'm not ready for a wife."

"Today you laugh," Hyman said. "Tomorrow you'll wrack your brains out to get some man's daughter to say yes to you."

"I won't say I won't play a little here and there. But I have to learn, then I have to go to Israel. Maybe then I'll be ready for a wife."

"And when do you expect that to be?"

"Ask my teacher. He's the expert." Alcohol had lowered Shimshon's restraint. "We didn't have it easy starting to talk. I'm so glad sandwiches and fruit helped. I really appreciate your teaching. But that makes me wonder even more who you are and where you come from."

"I come from the planet Uranus," Hyman said. "The real question is why what I'm teaching you isn't enough lately?"

"I practice! You've seen how late I stay."

"I also see the disappointment in your face."

Shimshon shifted uneasily. "Shouldn't practice have made my work a little smoother and faster by now?"

"When you practice as hard as you play it may. Perhaps you should find yourself a teacher who doesn't care how much you drink and how you spend your time."

"Come on! I don't want anyone but you to teach me."

"Then concentrate or I won't be teaching you much longer." Hyman adjusted his shirtsleeves. "Stop thinking rules and straight lines. They won't help you master Victor or learn accounting. All you need is time. Time, patience and sobriety."

Shimshon surveyed the polished top of Hyman's desk, the black ledger books stacked in the corner, the straw-colored worksheets, the bare walls, the tattered overcoat. He studied Hyman's hands as if he were asking how many years' practice had been ground into those fingers. Ten? Had practice aged their skin and gnarled their joints? His eyes followed the thin tendons over Hyman's knuckles, past blue veins and up his slender wrists. Rubbing his own left wrist, Shimshon might have thought about the way Hyman talked of a machine's rhythm as if he were riding a Thoroughbred. Maybe he thought, Hyman's fingers are so thin compared to mine. And his wrists are a third the size. But after you get under the shirtcuffs, we have one very important thing in common. Between us we have ten blue numbers that intrude into every conversation we have. "You amaze me," Shimshon said. "Your hands work like none I've ever seen."

"Practice. I've just practiced a lot."

"It's more than practice. You understand your work so well, you could teach it to an infant."

"To an infant definitely not." A faint smile creased the corners of Hyman's eyes. "To a nine-year-old, maybe."

"When Sam told me how good you were, I never imagined he might be understating." Shimshon leaned across the desk. "I worry I won't ever be half as good as you."

Hyman looked stunned. "I thought you figured you were already better than everyone." He paused as if pondering something unexpected. "Don't worry. With hard work and time you'll be twice as good."

"I'm not a natural like you."

"I'm no natural." Hyman laid his glasses on the desk. "Accounting came hard to me. I'm not the smartest either. In fact, I'm the one who took longest to learn."

"You don't have to lie to make me feel better."

"It's true. If a subject comes too fast, a man never really comprehends it. But if he struggled to learn what came easily to everyone else, he knows it inside out." Hyman looked tense, and rubbed his hands together. "That's the beauty of bookkeeping," he said, and put his glasses back on. "It's perfectly logical. If you study it thoroughly, what you find never surprises you. But for today, the lesson's over. Talk is cheap. You can't depend on words. But when you have dollars on your Victor, you have real numbers that will be the same tomorrow as they are today."

"How could I forget?" Shimshon said.

"Pay careful attention. Every ledger has to balance. Debits and credits have to match."

"I heard you the fiftieth time. Whenever I ask the simplest question about the man I eat lunch with every day, you change the subject and tell me for the fifty-first time that credits and debits have to match."

"And I'll repeat that message until I'm absolutely convinced that you don't need to hear it again." The bells of St. Anne's rang twelve forty-five and started playing "Ave

Maria." "Just keep practicing. You'll be there sooner than you think."

After Shimshon had left, Hyman focused on Ajax Lace, whose computations engrossed him until two thirty, when the typewriters and adding machines silenced for the afternoon coffee break. Words like "such a taste" and "delicious" reached Hyman's ears. But he concentrated on work until he was so thoroughly absorbed that seductive words and aromas were excluded from the single beam of attention he fixed on Victor. Deeply absorbed, Hyman did not hear the sound of footsteps coming down the corridor toward him. Nor did he consciously register that they had stopped right outside. He even remained oblivious to the first knocks on the glass outside his cubicle. When the second round of knocks came, he perceived some remote annoyance, a hammer thudding in the distance. He merely shifted in his chair and kept working. But when the third round came, loud and insistent, a gavel calling for attention, his concentration broke.

"Go away, Shimshon," he said and continued working.

"Mr. Schwartz?" a woman replied.

Hyman turned around and saw Faye Sondheimer.

She took two hesitant steps in and put a cup of coffee and a little bag on the desk. "I hope you enjoy it. I made it myself. Happy Hanukkah, Mr. Schwartz," Faye said and hurried away.

Inside the bag, Hyman found a thick piece of coffee cake. She bakes the way a Jewish man likes, he thought, with sugar and cinnamon sprinkled on top. Would Rachel think I was disloyal if I tasted it, or would she say that chances come too rarely for a man to refuse good food?

Hyman brought the cake to his lips. Sweet aromas of cinnamon penetrated his sinuses. The cake tasted more delicious than it smelled; jam and sweet dough melted in his mouth. When he tasted Mrs. Sondheimer's cake, he remembered that Rachel's cakes were the best.

He savored another bite. Pleasure shut his eyes. When

Rachel baked, our apartment smelled like a pâtisserie. Hyman sipped the coffee and took more cake. Do you remember, Rachel? I see you as if we were together today. You're pulling a cake sheet covered with honey-gold *tzviebachs* out of the oven. Hyman took another bite and smelled. When you baked, our house smelled like heaven.

Hyman actually felt like he was back in Warsaw watching Rachel put the cakes on his kitchen table. But in his mind's eye, Faye stepped in front of Rachel and offered Hyman a slice. She grew larger; her smile turned grotesque and transformed into a harlequin's leer. Hyman opened his eyes, threw the last bite of cake and the empty coffee cup into his trash can. Rachel. How can I lie and say you would be happy? I shouldn't enjoy a strange woman's cake when you can't enjoy cakes anymore. He scratched his left hand. I'm not blind, Rachel. Mrs. Sondheimer would bring me more cakes if I wanted. But I know how one piece of cake leads to a coffee and then to a date. She makes me think about those possibilities. But then I'd be saying that you won't ever come back. I promised on our wedding night that we would be forever. And when I promise once, I don't change my mind.

Chapter Eighteen

THAT EVENING Hyman walked uptown past shoppers, tourists, cops, carolers, Santas asking for donations and lines of tiny white lights scurrying up Gimbel's sides. A light snow fell. Hyman spotted a few young boys gathered in front of a Macy's display window and became curious. "Please tell Dad to get me one," he heard a boy say. "Please Mom. I've been good all year."

Hyman looked in the window and saw a Lionel locomotive spewing steam, pulling a tapeworm of rolling stock around a track: two New Haven Railroad passenger cars with a row of soft yellow lights running along their sides led the way. After them came a gleaming dining car. A soot-blackened Erie & Lackawanna car brimming over with coal and two maroon cattle cars whose sliding doors were chained shut followed. Then came a long car with a flat bed; its siderails held in a stack of long logs. Last was a bright red caboose that seemed to be scurrying to keep up.

The locomotive snaked down a hillside. A speaker in the window's upper corner broadcast the sounds of the action. The locomotive blew its whistle, accelerated on the flats, and rushed past furrowed green fields, plastic trees, people and barns, past flashing red lights, ringing bells and striped barriers.

"Pleasantville, next stop," a voice shouted. As the train

pulled into an American Gothic Station, a whistle blew, a calliope started playing and a carousel in the background began to circle. The train stopped. "All off," the loudspeaker announced. "All off for Pleasantville."

A plastic station master stood on the platform and swivelled robotically, as if welcoming debarking passengers. At the same time a derrick lowered a hook toward the flatbed car's timbers.

My father sold wood, Hyman thought. He loaded logs in Ravaruska and shipped them to Germany for telephone poles. In the summer, Papa took me to the station. What talks we had. He was proud that he was making the family's wood business bigger. But while we waited for the train, Papa told me stories about what he really loved, about Vienna and Paris. He talked about them as if they were another world, a magical planet where Jews could learn science and mathematics.

"Please," Hyman heard the boy ask his mother as the Lionel pulled out of "Pleasantville" and started around the circuit again. "Please tell Dad to keep his promise. Last year he said if I was good, he would buy me a train set."

Why should a boy have to beg? Hyman thought. If David were alive, before he even asked I would buy him a Lionel, no questions asked. We would set it up and order it around. Pick up wood! Drop it off! Get into those hills for more! I'd give anything to have one chance to tell David how once upon a time Schwartz was a big name in the wood business.

The maroon cattle car sped past the window. An image flashed through Hyman's mind: the cattle car that took him to Auschwitz. You never have to worry where a Lionel will take you, he thought. You tell Lionels where to go, not vice versa.

Hyman wiped a melting snowflake off his glasses. Putting his glasses back on he recalled how he had made Hanukkah of 1941 a miracle. Even though David wasn't even six yet, he already knew how hard life was and never asked "What will you bring me?" But I kept hunting all over the ghetto for

111

some present. When I came into the apartment on Hanukkah eve, David was so involved in stacking blocks he didn't
even hear me. So I hid the box behind my back and said
"Happy Hanukkah." My David ran to me; his blanket fell off
his shoulders. He threw his arms around my neck and when
I said, "Guess what, my little *bochar?*" David smiled and
opened the box. He loved his present so much he put it right
on to be warm. If it had been 1938, when we still had an
apartment to ourselves and money to burn, I could buy him
a Lionel ten times as big as the one in Macy's window. But
in 1941, the son of Hyman Schwartz, scion of the Rava
Schwartz family, jumped up and down because for Hanukkah I found him one used overcoat.

Papa always said that life goes in cycles. Wood that's cheap
today will be dear tomorrow. But Papa also said you can
count on one more thing. That the day after tomorrow wood
will be cheap again. Papa knew about wood, not about people. Because for David life was a straight line. You're born,
you die, and after that there's nothing.

Hyman turned back to Macy's window. The train again
pulled into Pleasantville, the calliope played, the carousel
circled, the plastic conductor waved, the whistle blew and a
puff of smoke furled out of the locomotive's smokestack.

Couldn't God have given human beings cycles too?

Hyman headed uptown, thinking about the boys clumped
together, their noses pressed against Macy's window. He
chastised their parents for ignoring how lucky they were.
You have sons. Why make them beg? He walked into the
Excelsior thinking, I would never make David beg. But as
he started up the stairs, a second voice inside his head dis-
sented: That isn't true. Now that you have no son to lose,
you brag about what a good father you would have been. But
if you're so generous, why do you make Shimshon beg for
every little thing?

I don't make him beg, Hyman retorted as he reached the
top of the first flight of stairs.

Oh, don't you? He asks you a question as simple as "Where

do you come from?" and you change the subject. You never give him what he wants unless he begs.

That's not true. But as Hyman headed up the second flight of stairs, he wondered, Do I really make Shimshon beg?

There's no question about whether you do. Every few days you threaten to stop teaching him. The only question is why?

Because I don't really want to teach him. I'd rather be alone, Hyman thought. I teach him as a special thanks to Mr. Teitlebaum. Heading up the final flight, Hyman looked at the carpet runner erased by wear, and thought, This place is old, this carpet's old, and I'm too old to fool myself. So what if I teach Shimshon because he reminds me of what David might have been?

Inside, Hyman surveyed his room. The mahogany table was more chipped, the walls were bare, and the chair's velvet seat had worn down to the canvas.

Now you're beginning to understand, Hyman. To a man who has so little, a student can be very important.

But I don't want him to be. Hyman sat in his chair and pondered. After losing David I swore never to have anyone; losing what you love hurts too much. So why should I consider throwing away my resolution for a Hungarian *mamzer* who only reminds me of my son? What if he leaves?

What do you mean *if* he leaves?

Exactly that! What will I do if he moves to Israel?

If he moves to Israel isn't the question. The only question is *when*.

But he has so much to learn.

And if you teach him, he'll learn quickly. Shimshon's smart. Criticize a thousand fathers you never met. Then stand in front of a mirror, look at how you make Shimshon beg every day and ask yourself what Hyman Schwartz really would have done if his son were alive.

Hyman rested his forehead on the window glass and looked at the polished uptown windows that had warm yellow light streaming out. He imagined the happy people in those apartments who soon would be celebrating Hanukkah with potato pancakes, apple sauce and chocolate money. Snowflakes drifting past looked like falling tears. Is it different when you have a son? Do you have to make him beg? The windows answered with a silent glow.

I know a man who had a son who grew up, Hyman thought. He sighed deeply and closed his eyes. He's the only person I can really ask. Hyman knew that the voice he had heard in his head had been that man's. Tell me Papa. Would you make Shimshon beg?

The gray emptiness in Hyman's mind cleared and he saw his father standing on an unpaved Ravaruska street, staring at the ground, his hands clasped behind his back.

Papa looked up and spoke: "I told you once, Hyman. I'm yesterday. You have to be tomorrow."

How can I be tomorrow if I haven't got a son?

"You've got Shimshon. What's wrong with him?"

He's not my flesh and blood.

"Why should that make a difference? He's got no one; you've got no one. Why not teach him?"

Because he'll go to Israel and I'll have no one again. What will I do then Papa?

"What every man does. I told you we have to sacrifice so the next generation would live like normal people."

But my son's dead Papa. There is no next generation.

"We come naked into this world. We leave it naked too. If you won't create the next generation, at least educate it."

Hyman was stunned. Now he comprehended: Papa. When you said that I had to leave Rava so your son would never become an old Jew who prayed all day for the Messiah, why didn't you look me straight in the eye? For a long time, I was angry with you. But tonight, I understand that you couldn't look at me because losing your son hurt too much. Maybe we were lucky Papa. Because the war came, you and I never had to meet in Warsaw, never had to sit across a table stammering because we had nothing to say to one another. You say, "Treat Shimshon like a son. Stop making him beg." But

114

he's not my son. He's a stranger. Hyman paused for a second and covered his eyes. It's not true Papa. He's no stranger anymore. The more time I spend with him, the more I like him. Then I teach him and know that each lesson pushes him one step closer to leaving.

"It doesn't push him, Hyman. It helps him."

Does that mean I should answer his questions?

Hyman felt a disapproving silence fill the room.

Oh I know exactly what you think Papa. A student is the same as a son to a man who is childless. Even if it cuts you in two, you have to do what you know is right. If you don't help a son grow up, you'll never forgive yourself for trying to cripple him. Even if he doesn't hate you, you'll hate yourself. For your own good, don't make him beg.

Hyman settled back in his chair. Having communed with his father and understood the sacrifice he had made, Hyman decided that in the coming months he would answer all of Shimshon's questions.

Answer his questions! Immediately Hyman felt liberated. He no longer would have to be vigilant for every nuance that suggested intimacy. He was free—he would do what every good father had to: he would teach Shimshon and, when the right time came, he would let him go. The decision resolved the question that had bedeviled Hyman. Now I know what men are good for: for being used. And I know what a man should do before he dies. He should give all he's learned, no strings attached, to a young man who can use it. Commitment is what allows a man to look death in the eyes without flinching.

Hyman pushed himself out of his chair, walked to his closet and pulled his manila envelope out of the blanket. Embracing the envelope in his arms, he thought, You would agree that I shouldn't make the boy beg, don't you Rachel? Please remember. Now I'll need you more than ever. I'll need you to remind me that what I'm doing is right. And when Shimshon leaves, I'll need your smile to keep me warm. Help me, Rachel. Help me be as strong as Papa was the day he walked me to the railway station and said good-bye. I was hurt that Papa sent me away, saying "What could you learn by me? To sell wood at a profit?" I never understood how sad he must have felt watching my train pull away.

Hyman cried himself to sleep that night. And for the first time since arriving at the Excelsior, he slept soundly and felt refreshed when he awoke the next morning.

Chapter Nineteen

HEAVY SNOWS that began just before Christmas had buried New York City. Garbage trucks with huge blades mounted on their front ends plowed the downfall into high mounds; other trucks sprayed salt and sand on major thoroughfares. The tires of passing cars spewed grit and turned the snow-white mounds black. By New Year's the roads were slushy. Buses and the subway ran with long delays.

When work resumed, everyone was late coming in. Everyone but Hyman, that is. Despite bleakness and frigid air, Hyman felt revitalized as he walked to Teitlebaum & Sharfenstein. Since he had resolved to answer Shimshon's questions, biting winds only braced him for the future.

Throughout January, Shimshon dedicated himself to learning. When he asked a question, Hyman answered graciously. But Shimshon, preoccupied with accounting, asked only questions having to do with the work; none about Hyman himself.

Hyman was relieved. Shimshon's absorption allowed him a short reprieve to enjoy teaching. He knew that once Shimshon became secure enough to begin asking personal questions again, the boy would be on the road to self-sufficiency and to moving on.

Hyman paid more careful attention to how Shimshon worked and was surprised that he had been blind to the

117

obvious; like him, Shimshon was a perfectionist. One lunch-time late in January, Shimshon slapped Victor's side. "This steel son of a bitch is driving me crazy."

"You're driving yourself crazy. Victor's a dumb animal. Like a horse, the second he throws you off, you have to climb back on."

"You've got him wrong, Mr. Schwartz. Victor's a mean bastard."

"He's dumber than a horse. He can't even move without a man on top telling him what to do. Go easy on yourself. You have to walk before you can gallop," Hyman said. "Don't worry. You're getting there."

"Like hell I am." Despite his frustration, Shimshon persisted, staying late every night, calculating and recalculating worksheets, going through different strategies for minimizing taxes. By February's third week, he had mastered the operation of the adding machine; Victor's handle rarely jammed, his number keys never stuck, and paper never got knotted in the spool or tangled in the rachets.

Hyman was pleased that Shimshon had persisted. By late February, his progress was obvious. "You're getting good on Victor," Hyman said to him one day. "The sound of your work shows me you're close."

Shimshon picked a pencil off of Hyman's desktop and drummed the rhythm with its eraser. "Doesn't that sound right? Some days I'm convinced I feel the rhythm. But the next day I'm all thumbs. Maestro Schwartz," he went on, pointing at Victor with the pencil. "Will you play this Stradivarius?"

"I'm not showing off. When I came here I struggled for over a year to get to be as good as you are after just three and a half months."

"You should have had my teacher." Shimshon handed a worksheet to Hyman. "Show me again, maestro."

Hyman began computing. Numbers raced through his fingers. Several times he had to lean closer to the worksheet to read Shimshon's handwriting, but like a violinist deeply immersed in music, Hyman constantly coordinated the rhythm with the forward and backward lean of his head and shoulders. The performance was virtuoso.

When Hyman reached the middle of the worksheet, Shimshon glanced at his wristwatch. "How do you do it?"

Hyman answered without breaking his rhythm. "Don't ask me, ask my fingers." He computed steadily until he finished the worksheet.

"Yeah!" Shimshon shouted and checked his watch again. "I worked fifteen minutes to compute this page. You finished in under three."

Hyman saw the look of admiration in Shimshon's eyes and thought, Isn't that the way a son looks at his father? "I once hated my Victor too. Since I could do the work better in my head, I hated being forced to use a machine."

"Who forced you?"

"Mr. Teitlebaum said he needed written records. So I practiced for a very long time until instead of slowing me down, Victor helped me move faster. But I'll tell you a secret. No matter what Mr. Teitlebaum says he needs, I still check everything in my head."

"If you'll forgive me for asking, Mr. Schwartz, I've always been curious to know how you learned to count so quickly in your head."

"Lots of people count quickly in their head," Hyman snapped. But then he remembered his resolution. Sitting silently in his chair, he searched for the accurate answer. "I'm good with numbers because I've been practicing since I was a boy. When I was no more than four or five, I took walks with my father and he would ask, 'So how much is two plus three?' Papa was so happy when I got the answer right that I kept solving even harder problems. My father used to say, 'With such a good head you're really going to be somebody.' "

Hyman's answer, opening the first closed door to his past, seemed to startle Shimshon. He sat silently for a moment as if pondering whether to go further. "Where did you grow up?" he finally said.

Hyman put his head in his hands, and stared at the floor. I've started, he thought. There's no turning back. Stay beside me, Rachel. Straightening up, Hyman looked directly at Shimshon. "When you were growing up in Budapest, did anyone tell you about the shtetl?"

Shimshon nodded, silently, gently, amazement at Hyman's sudden willingness to be open etched into the creases of his forehead.

"I grew up in a little shtetl in Galicia. Ravaruska was its name. We may both be Jews and may both have been in camps, but where I started and where you did were worlds apart. Rava was a shtetl in the eastern part of the Austrian empire. I was an only child born when my parents were already pretty old. Papa loved to tell stories. One of his favorites was about taking Mama to see the professor in Vienna to find out why she didn't get pregnant. The doctor put her in the hospital for three weeks to study her condition. Those three weeks changed Papa's life, because one night he had an adventure which Mama would have talked him out of if she hadn't been in the hospital.

"Until 1918, your Budapest was one of the empire's two great cities, it and Vienna. And it remained a great city afterward. So it would be hard for you to imagine that in the first years of the twentieth century, my father's great, risqué adventure was going to see the Vienna theater perform *Hamlet*. The very Orthodox never saw plays or read novels. To them, Shakespeare and Goethe were as unkosher as pork. So for Papa to go to the theater was outright rebellion.

"After that night, Papa was a divided man; his brain knew that the very religious lived like moles, burying themselves underground. He used to say that his trip to Vienna brought civilization to the Schwartz family. But personally, he still dressed and lived like the extremely religious. Mama saw the trip differently. She said they came to Vienna because she was sick. By the time they left, Papa's brain had been infected with *goyishe* germs.

"The day after the play, Papa bought thirty books, some

about biology, others filled with pictures of birds, trees, flowers, and his favorite, wild animals. Like all Jews in Rava, Papa knew the Bible stories backward and forward. But he wanted more. 'Even Adam knew the name of every living thing. Why should Jews in this day know less?' Papa used to say."

Hyman's mind began to wander. He visualized the tall wooden bookcase filled with wonderful, mysterious tomes: geography books full of mind-bogging photographs of cities like Vienna, Paris, Berlin, even New York. He recalled his father's love for books with pictures of the animals of Europe, Africa and America. And Hyman's father had a special reverence for Goethe, Shakespeare, and Schiller. "Although Papa never got back to Vienna, he paid that bookseller to send him a dozen new books a year. From a university's point of view, Papa's knowledge was superficial, maybe even pedestrian. But those books and what he saw in them probably meant more to Papa than books mean to most professors. In Ravaruska, his was the only library that had a bookcase full of what the very religious called unkosher books."

Hyman looked at Shimshon. When he saw he was listening with rapt attention, he went on more confidently. "Papa stayed Orthodox, but hated superstition. 'That's for Hasidim,' he used to say. The Hasidim in our area believed that the rabbi of Belz, a shtetl a few miles from Rava, was midway between God and man. 'Treating a man like he's the intermediary to God is a Catholic idea,' Papa said. 'The Belzer Hasidim believe that the rebbe does magic, that he can intercede with God. Backward they look. We Schwartzes have to look to the future—zoology, biology, chemistry, physics, and the jewel of science, mathematics. Those Hasidim are so irrational they won't eat tomatoes because they say they're unkosher apples.'

"My Papa was a man with convictions. 'I can't worry about evil eyes,' he used to say when everyone in town feared them. His beliefs left him without close friends in Rava.

"Students flocked to the rebbe of Belz from all over Eu-

rope. After the First World War, during the rebellions and upheaval after the empire collapsed, hundreds came from Budapest alone hoping that maybe they'd see the rebbe's face. To a nonbeliever, he was just a short, religious man with a white beard and blue eyes that looked right through you. But to Belzer Hasidim, seeing the rebbe was standing as close as a mortal could to God's throne. If a piece of bread fell from the rebbe's mouth, ten students dove under the table, clamoring to get to it first, to eat a crust that had touched the rebbe's lips," Hyman said, noticing Shimshon's disbelieving look. "No, I'm not exaggerating. Those Belzer Hasidim may have been Torah scholars. But they were also zealots who lived in the Middle Ages. I once asked a Hasid why he went to the rebbe. He smiled and answered as if I was stupid for not seeing what was obvious: 'So maybe I can learn how he laces his shoes.'

"I started practicing numbers in Rava when Papa and I took walks. He believed mathematics was the pinnacle of knowledge. 'So how much is two plus three, Hyman?' he asked when I was a very little boy. The older I got, the more complicated the problems became. Papa and I took walks all year round."

Hyman remembered the walks. Even when the snows were melting or when rains turned Rava's streets into mud seas, father and son bundled up, put on boots that reached above their knees, and walked. But more than questions filled their time together. Hyman remembered balancing on his father's lap and studying pictures in the foreign books. In this way, he learned about the natural world surrounding them. His mother would complain bitterly that Hyman's head was being filled with nonsense, but he knew that his father was sharing what he loved.

"When I got older, I asked my father why he worked in the wood business. I remember his downcast face as he answered me. 'It's a living. My father was in the wood business. What choice did I have? Sure, thank God I can afford what no one else in Rava can. And you could make the busi-

ness bigger, Hyman. But you would always belong to this little town's merchant world.'

"Papa wanted a different life for me. 'You could be somebody living somewhere,' he told me a hundred times. 'Franz Joseph made sure that a Jew can get out of Ravaruska. Go to university, Hyman.' When we were home, he sometimes pointed to a picture in one of his books. 'Have you ever seen a building that tall in Rava? In Vienna, in Warsaw, in Berlin you'll see so many six-story buildings, you'll be proud that science does so much for us. If already now the Eiffel Tower is almost a quarter of a mile high, can you imagine what buildings will look like in fifty years?' Papa became poetic. 'They'll stretch to the sky and kiss the heavens. God's angels will dance on their roofs and sing from their spires.'

"Mama said that like the builders of the Tower of Babel, those scientists were leading us to doom. When Mama spoke that way, Papa ignored her and acted like she wasn't there. The older I got, the more he said, 'Forget what Mama tells you about this village. Get out of Rava. If you stay here you'll be a field mouse poking through blades of grass and thinking he's pushing aside oaks. Go to Warsaw. If you want to be king of the beasts, go to Vienna!'

I didn't want to leave Rava, so right after my bar mitzvah, I asked Papa to teach me. 'What should I teach you? To sell wood at a profit? You'll get out of here, Hyman. You'll go to university. You'll be the first Schwartz to become somebody.'

"To teach me, Papa hired the only tutor for secular subjects in all Rava. A year before I left town, I asked Papa, 'If I go to Warsaw, I'll learn mathematics and physics and chemistry. Will we have anything left to talk about when we take walks?'

"It's only lately that I can understand what the sadness in his eyes should have told me then. But I was too young to really comprehend. 'You're a smart boy, Hyman. When Franz Joseph said we could live like everybody else, he didn't add that by freeing Jews he condemned every progressive father in Galicia to sacrifice his relationship with his son. A few years from now, I'll still be in the old world. You'll be in the new. That's how it has to be. Accept destiny, Hyman. Because of it your son and grandson and Schwartzes ever after will be part of a world where Jews are normal people. It's high time!' "

Hyman went on to tell Shimshon how his parents' marriage, like all the marriages of that epoch and locale, had been arranged. His father described his excitement when he first saw Mama under the wedding canopy, so thin and beautiful. " 'She was as delicate as a rose in the first days of spring,' he once said to me. 'Unfortunately, over the seasons, delicate flowers wilt, petals fall off. With age, whatever was beautiful because it was delicate becomes frail.'

"All the years I was growing up, Mama was sick on and off. Papa said he was surprised when her sickness started a few months after they married. She was so sick after I was born that Papa hired a Polish woman named Wanda, who raised me for almost two years. Papa said I really loved that Wanda, but I can't even remember what she looked like. When Mama's joints didn't hurt anymore and she could get out of bed, Papa sent the woman home. Whenever Mama became sick again, which was often, Papa did the cooking. In our town, a father who cooked was unheard-of."

Sitting there speaking to Shimshon, Hyman recalled the taste of his father's matzoh balls, light as feathers in the chicken soup, and the rich aroma of cholent full of barley, beans, potatoes and chunks of beef simmering on the oven's fire for hours on end.

Nearly overwhelmed, Hyman sat still, his eyes closed, as he replayed in his mind the day he left Rava for good. His father walked to the station with him. It was early fall; his breath froze in the cold air. Ten minutes before the train was to leave, they stood at the station waiting for his mother. With five minutes left, she still hadn't come.

Now in New York so many years later, tears welled in Hyman's eyes again as he recalled his frantic search for his mother. He felt his father hug him again. He could hear the train's whistle blow and felt his father let go and carry the satchel up the train's iron steps.

"Where's Mama?" Hyman muttered out loud, and slumped forward in his chair.

He startled Shimshon, who must have realized that Hyman's silence and shut eyes meant that Hyman was lost in his reminiscences. St. Anne's bells rang the three-quarter hour, but neither man stirred. Shimshon sat patiently and waited for Hyman to break the silence again.

Hyman gradually sat back. He remembered hearing his mother calling him and watching her run up to the train out of breath. She handed him a rolled-up newspaper as the whistle blew again. "I made this for you," she said as steam from the engine drifted past them. "I'm afraid the chicken got a little overcooked and dried, but it's still good for you." That's how Hyman remembered his mother. Dried and good for you, never delightful and tasty, had to be good enough.

"Anyway, the last time I saw Rava was the day I left for the university. The train's whistle blew, the wheels screeched and began to roll. I jumped onto the train, and waved good-bye.

" 'I'm yesterday!' Papa shouted after me. 'You have to be tomorrow.' "

Hyman told Shimshon that he had shoved his valise under a seat and stared out the thick glass window. All the Jewish people were in shops selling or in yeshivoth studying. When the train passed peasants working the countryside, Hyman noticed that without his knowing exactly why, the sight made tears run down his face.

The train snaked through the countryside rattling, shaking, wriggling from side to side on tracks that paralleled a dirt road. Fields rushed past. Fields and orchards, fields and orchards.

Hyman told Shimshon that he had been the only boy in town who had spent five years studying with a tutor, and the first to leave for university. "Can you even imagine it? Not one person in all the fields and orchards we passed had finished even ten years of school. By twelve or thirteen they had to slave full-time in the fields just so their families could stay alive.

"We eat well here, but Poland was always close to famine." Hyman described the weather on the day he left Rava. The sky boiled with thick, dark clouds. Farmers knew that clouds like those could dump early snows that killed every cucumber, tomato and squash. If no thaw came, the root crops would be buried too. By March, half the peasants in Lvov province would have empty root cellars. So men, women, boys and girls, every peasant in Poland who could still use a shovel, drive a cart, or climb a ladder was harvesting. In field after field, wagons drove on unpaved roads or rode along the tops of the wide dirt mounds that separated the orchards from one another, stopping every twenty feet to let babushka'd women unload bushels of harvest into the wagons' flat beds. Then it continued along the mound while sighing women rushed back to the fields and orchards for more.

Strong men dug pitchforks into the sides of furrows, twisted them hard and pushed them from side to side to loosen the earth. Women crawled on their knees and dug their fingers through soil to get radishes, turnips, carrots and even potatoes just in case the snows were so heavy that they did not melt until spring. Children climbed high ladders and reached their hands through dark red leaves to pick apples, cherries and pears. Winter was coming.

"When a fifth set of tracks drew closer to my train window only a few kilometers outside Warsaw, I finally began to realize that a big city really was different from a shtetl. In Rava, we had a week of parties when we got our one set of tracks. But here tracks surrounded my train and streamed to Warsaw. In Rava tracks meant people could travel and that a businessman like Papa could send logs to Germany. What did it mean that Warsaw needed a field full of tracks?"

That afternoon, Hyman passed full trains and empty trains, idle locomotives, black mountains of coal, signalmen, brakemen, engineers and stevedores arguing about boxcars that needed unloading. In his first ten minutes in Warsaw's trainyard, he saw more trains just standing idle than he had seen moving in all the rest of his life.

And steam. The station he pulled into was a gigantic steam bath. Rava's station was a dollhouse compared to Warsaw's. When he stepped down the metal stairs and stood on the platform, he just stared, following with his eyes plumes of steam that rose more than sixty feet to the curved glass ceiling. Porters rolling baggage bumped him. Stevedores unloading sacks of grain jostled him.

Hyman saw more marvels that day. A chauffeur in a black cap and white gloves waited on the ramp at attention. When his boss came, the chauffeur whipped off his cap and bowed. "Yes, sir. So good to see you, sir. The carriage is waiting, sir!" Vendors carrying baskets tugged at Hyman's sleeve. "Wouldn't your mouth water for a herring? No. How about an onion roll or piroshki?"

"Shimshon," Hyman said. "If Papa hadn't arranged for the relative of a man we knew in Rava to pick me up, I would have stood there for hours just watching.

" 'Schwartz. Hyman Schwartz,' I heard a man yelling. I carried my valise over and introduced myself. You wouldn't call his greeting a welcome. The relative was a cold man with a job to do. He told me who he was and said he had been hired to drive me to the room he had rented in a house near the university."

For his first three years in Warsaw, Hyman studied in his room most of the time. But he told Shimshon that after he met the woman who would be his wife in 1933, he *really* began to see the wondrous city he was in. It hurt him to talk about Rachel, but since he had said he would, he went on. Rachel had made him see the enormous parks filled with roses, carnations, crocuses, tulips, irises, with grass as green as emeralds and as thick as Persian rugs. Warsaw's town square, Stare Miasto, was ancient, built when the Jews were still in Spain. "Can you imagine what a cathedral looked like to a twenty-two-year-old boy from the shtetl who shivered every time he walked past a church?"

Hyman said that without Rachel he never would have paid attention to doormen at elegant cafés. She pointed out their scarlet uniforms with gold braiding. "Why dress like that just to open doors for rich people?" she had whispered to him when she was just his girlfriend.

"But Rachel didn't just criticize. She really appreciated European culture." He told how she recognized and could sing songs that played from a hundred Warsaw steeples. Because Hyman felt at home around farmers, she showed him an enormous market where farmers' carts, identical to the one Thaddeus had been driving, came to sell produce. Some Saturdays they went there just to watch farmers unload bright red tomatoes, little cucumbers to be made into pickles, huge pale-green cabbages for sauerkraut, and white cauliflowers big as sheep heads.

"Jews in Rava spoke Polish, Ukrainian and Yiddish. Rachel knew Polish and Yiddish, but she understood French, Russian and English, too. And just from the accent she could tell southern Germans from northern, and Austrians from all the rest. She even spoke a little Hungarian, even though she was Galician on both sides. And she had a Leica camera to take pictures, and a light meter. Can you imagine? She even taught me to use it.

"After we married, we got an apartment where there happened to be a doctor's office in the same building. Someone who grew up in Budapest can't really understand how I felt having a doctor that close. Until the train came to Rava, if you needed a doctor, you had to take a wagon to Lvov. In 1900, my grandfather died of a ruptured appendix. He may have been big in the wood business, but that didn't help his appendix. By the time they got him to Lvov, it was too late to operate. His appendix had burst and his fever was a hundred six. Two days later he died. That would never have happened in Warsaw. Doctors' offices were everywhere. So were lawyers' and engineers'. There were businesspeople all over Warsaw who were so rich that Papa was a pauper next to them. Mansions, I tell you. Mansions. With tall white columns in front and butlers serving Scotch on the veranda. No one in Rava had ever tried Scotch. Vodka they knew. Slivovitz they knew. But Scotch?

"I had one friend at the university, Yossel, a student of politics and history. The university was filled with anti-Semites. A few months after I met Rachel, Professor Minkowski took me aside. 'Your work is promising,' he whispered as if he didn't want anyone to overhear. Then he stood erect and adjusted his suit. A disgusted look came to his face. Maybe you've seen it, the one when an anti-Semite turns away his nose like he just smelled shit. 'It's a pity that a man with such talent has to be a Jew.' "

Hyman described the university ironically as one big happy family where the highest intellectual principles governed. At examination time, a few boys from anti-Semitic clubs got together. Carrying tall poles with beautifully colored satin coats of arms tied near their tops, they marched, singing patriotic songs as their banners flapped in the breeze. They prayed that God or a new king would bless them with a Poland free of Jews. "I guess God heard *their* prayers."

"You still believe in God?" Shimshon interrupted.

"I keep my ledgers balanced. If He's so great, why aren't His?

"But, let's not talk nonsense, Shimshon. I want to tell you what happened to my friend Yossel. During the 1935 exam period he had trouble from one parade. Ten boys came up to him. 'Let's see whether anything's missing under your zipper, Yid,' their leader said. When Yossel started to walk away, they surrounded and grabbed him. He fought, but it was ten to one. They roughed him up, broke a few ribs and two of his fingers. They spread his legs and kicked his genitals. 'Maybe that will help what's missing grow back,' the leader laughed. Yossel was crumpled on the ground but was too proud to cry or groan. He just clenched his teeth and never said a word.

"Most of us figured that if we just kept quiet, danger would pass. We were like the opossum I read about in Papa's books. Bad times come. Bad times go. Like Papa had taught me, if wood's cheap today, tomorrow it will be expensive. Who imagined that Hitler would end all cycles?"

"That's why I'm moving to Israel," Shimshon said. "If Jews had fought, those bastards would never have picked on your Yossel."

Hyman looked at Shimshon like he was crazy. "You say! But what you want to believe won't change facts. You can't fight artillery with morality. Or even with kerosene bombs. Yossel was a fighter. Papa was a fighter. When it's ten to one and they have howitzers, it doesn't matter how hard you fight."

"Israel won a war against fifty to one," Shimshon said.

"In my math, fifty fighting Arabs equal one German with the runs," Hyman said. "Don't start with the propaganda. As a boy I heard enough big ideas from Papa.

"Sometimes I think that if Papa had moved to Warsaw, I would have been a lot happier. No matter how promising Minkowski or anyone else told me I was, learning mathematics was a struggle for me."

Hyman said that after he was six or seven, numbers meant nothing to him. But what they stood for and the world you could create from their symbols fascinated him. At university, he would sit under the kerosene lamp in his room until well past midnight trying to see what some formula looked like. He was never satisfied with knowing how to apply an equation. He needed to know how it fit into the entire mathematical world. He envied Einstein, who actually could visualize his relativity theories. Sometimes weeks after all the other students had finished with an equation, Hyman was still struggling to comprehend it. He thought that only if he could see it in his mind—not just the symbols mind you, but the picture its discoverer had had in his—would he really comprehend what a formula meant. To his way of thinking, if he finally did understand, he would be better off in the long run.

"That's what Papa told me I was working for: the long

run. And I trusted Papa. Even though I was studying much too hard to get back to Rava, I thought about Papa all the time. What would Papa say about this? What would Papa think about that? I missed his stories and his dreams for the future. My progress was slow. But Papa kept paying and never complained. 'Hasidic parents do as much for their Talmud students,' he said. 'Just finish,' was the only instruction he gave me during all those years.

"Even as a student I hated mistakes, flaws in the perfect mathematical world. Maybe when you're young you get an idea about the way things should be and after that, compromising seems like saying that the most perfect thing in the world is less than absolute. For me, other than in mathematics, really perfect happened only once, when I met Rachel.

"That was near the end of 1933. Yossel invited me to drink and schmooze with him at a café near the river. Yossel was from Cracow. For Hanukkah, his brother in Prague had sent him a tin of Virginia tobacco, a rare treat in 1933. Yossel rolled five cigarettes at our table, lit one, and puffed out blue-gray smoke. I remember everything about that night except what Yossel said. Like always, he was probably talking politics, which interested me about as much as smoking did.

"I remember sipping my Turkish coffee, and hearing a woman's voice say hello to Yossel, and his answer, 'Well, look who's here, and with two friends to boot.'

"I looked up. Through the smoke I saw the woman who had greeted Yossel lean down to whisper in his ear. The second woman had long blond hair, turquoise eyes, and would have passed for Christian anywhere. She was tapping her foot and eyeing every table, looking haughtily from one man to the next. But the first and second women didn't really matter because the third was my perfect. Even through that smoke I saw that her brown eyes were gentle, her face was pretty but not beautiful. Her dark hair brushed the shoulders of her blouse. She looked soft, the sort of person you just wanted to hug. When she saw me, she broke into a smile so convincing that I automatically had to smile back. And she wasn't smiling at every man, mind you—only at me. A handsome guy like you can't understand what that was like. Don't shake your head. Even women my age trip over themselves to be near you. But you wouldn't exactly call *me* a ladies' man.

"Courting Rachel wasn't as simple as finding a wife will be for you. In my family, every marriage before mine had been arranged. Sure, Papa had told me that a modern man had to choose his own wife, but no one ever taught me how. Luckily, Rachel wasn't afraid to be a little forward. Even that first day she herself asked whether she could join Yossel and me."

As they got to know one another, Hyman saw Rachel as someone from another world. Her grandfather had left the shtetl and moved to Cracow. Hyman had thought that Papa was a man of the world because he knew a few books. But Rachel's whole family went to concerts and knew about people he had never heard of: Rubens, Michelangelo, Rodin, and van Gogh. Rachel danced to Chopin and could whistle Beethoven. But she never made Hyman feel inferior. She liked what he knew about the old ways and got pleasure from seeing how excited he was to learn. She taught him about music and art, about how Warsaw worked, who its people were and where they came from.

"In the years we courted, I got my first education from professors. But I got my important education from Rachel. Maybe Papa's bookseller in Vienna brought culture to Abraham Schwartz, but Rachel Lebenthal brought life to Abraham's son.

"Rachel. I thought the happiest day of my life was the day I married her. But you know what happened a year later? Hyman Schwartz went and had himself a son."

"I'm afraid to ask, because I probably know the answer," Shimshon said. "But did you ever find out for sure what happened to them?"

"No, I didn't." Hyman fidgeted in his chair; the bells rang one forty-five. "I've been asking God that question for ten years and He's never answered." Hyman looked at the floor. "That's enough of a break for you. Let's get back to work."

Chapter Twenty

AS MARCH ENDED, New York's weather mellowed. Streets cleared, cars sparkled. But work at Teitlebaum & Sharfenstein intensified. Accountants rushed to finish ledgers and returns. Until tax day, Monday, April sixteenth, Hyman and Shimshon had less time to eat lunch together.

On April seventeenth, the pace at the office turned as relaxed as the gentle breeze outside and as rejuvenating as the warm rains seeping into Central Park's freshly thawed soil. In the park, sweet aromas of earth and peat moss suffused the air. Japanese cherry trees festooned themselves in clear pink blossoms for Passover seders and Easter festivities. In the breeze, petals and pollen swirling down from the trees looked like pink and white snow. Hyman and Shimshon returned to their old schedule.

By early May, pickup baseball players abounded on Hecksher Field. Laughing children rode on brightly painted horses that rounded the carousel as a calliope played "The Sidewalks of New York." And on May 9, 1956, Hyman finally confirmed that Shimshon had achieved the ultimate. "You feel it now. The rhythm's part of your fingers."

"Not really. I just do my work. And slowly."

"Speed's irrelevant this time of year. Even the slowest leave by five. Why hurry and cheat yourself? Enjoy the process. You'll move fast soon enough."

Shimshon stood and lowered his head. "And now for our sermon from Rabbi Schwartz. The first lesson, my dear congregants, is that you have to pay attention and go slowly." Shimshon sat down and spoke in a solemn, affected tone. "If you match your debits and credits now, dear friends, you won't have to spend weeks hunting for the simple mistakes that burden you. You won't berate yourself. 'Did I miss an obligation? Was there some mitzvah that should have shown up in my credit column or act of charity that I put aside out of laziness?' Let me warn you, dear friends . . ."

Hyman interrupted. "Make fun of yourself if you have to. But this strict teacher of yours knows how hard you've studied. Perfectionists don't get many opportunities to celebrate. Pat yourself on the back. You deserve it."

At ten in the morning on May twenty-fourth, the sun was already high above Broadway roofs, showering light through Sam's four tall windows. Sam stood in front of one, his hands pushed deep into his pants pockets. The long curtains billowed in the spring gusts. A knock on the door turned him around.

"You wanted to see me?" Shimshon said.

"I certainly did." Sam sat in the armchair and motioned Shimshon to the couch.

"Faye said we needed to discuss my work."

"Do we ever!" Sam lifted a stack of worksheets off the glass coffee table; bright sun reflected off the tabletop. "See these?"

Shimshon blinked and shaded his eyes.

"They're excellent!" Sam threw them on the table beside Shimshon. "Even after you persuaded Hyman to teach you, I never imagined you could learn so quickly. Your work is simply excellent, and not just because Hyman is teaching you. A good teacher can encourage a man to do his best, but he can't create talent, which you, my young friend, have plenty of."

"I have more to learn than Hyman has already forgotten."

"What Hyman obviously remembers makes it ridiculous to speculate about what he's forgotten." Sam pressed his right thumb and forefinger together. "You're not that much like Hyman. You're a doer like me. You won't spend your life focused on details."

"I won't go to Israel half-educated."

"How much better do you have to be? Rossberg thought your plan to account for damaged Persian lambskins was brilliant. And last week the Haskins and Sells auditor who does spot checks for me said that other than Hyman, you keep the finest books at this firm. You still need to pick up your speed substantially, but that's just a matter of practice and experience. Your ideas are novel and if your books stay this good until the end of June, I'm going to ask you to start checking Abromowitz's work."

Shimshon frowned.

"Only kidding. But after June thirtieth, Abromowitz will stop checking yours. You don't need his supervision anymore."

Shimshon stared at a silver cigarette box on the coffee table. "I still have a lot to learn, Sam. Can I stay a little longer?"

"You can stay for the next forty years if you'd like. But you're too ambitious to do it. The lessons you still have to learn come with experience, and if you plan to emigrate, you can only learn Israeli tax laws when you get there."

"But Hyman has shown me how much more there is to know."

"Compared to Hyman we all have more to know. As long as you try to learn everything he could teach you, you'll be staying right here. Because Hyman Schwartz won't ever leave New York City."

"You also said he wouldn't teach me. Some more time and he may just change his mind and go to Israel with me."

"Like that chair's going to do a jig." Sam leaned toward Shimshon and spoke in a quiet voice. "Do you think that spring follows every winter? Life and people don't work that way. Just because you got Hyman to teach you doesn't mean you can get him to deliver whatever you want."

The curtains over the windows billowed in the breeze.

"What are you really saying?" Shimshon asked.

Sam leaned back. "Hyman is a tenacious man. Tell him something once, and he'll hold you to it forever. Over ten years ago I told him that if I didn't have Sharp as a partner I wouldn't care how he dressed. Hyman saw through my 'I'm a good guy' ruse while I was still convinced that, like Jack Rossberg, I didn't judge anybody. His goddamned clothes belong on some hobo, not on the best-paid accountant here. But I gave him my word once and he's held me to it. Both because he's tenacious and because he needs to look like shit."

"We both know he must have troubles. But you promised him something and I didn't."

"Oh, didn't you? What about that you'd move to Israel?"

"That's fact, not promise."

"Anybody who knows Hyman knows that he's factored your leaving into his equation. So if you want to stay, please tell me now. I'll plan accordingly and sleep more easily. Because if Hyman wanted a shoulder to lean on, he would have gone home with Jack Rossberg last Yom Kippur."

"Rossberg's a stranger. When I first approached Hyman, I was a stranger too. But now Hyman's my best friend."

"You're a friend of one side of him. Why do young people forget history? This is the same Hyman Schwartz who screamed in synagogue until they had to carry him out. Do you think that kind of man changes in six months?"

"Almost eight."

"Almost eight. He's a volcano. And if he erupts, there won't be any glueing him together again." Exasperated, Sam paced the Tabriz carpet. "Do you really think that just because you're closer to being ready to leave, Hyman is?"

"I'm not ready."

"Go on! Get annoyed with me, Shimshon. Think that I'm

136

worried about losing a worker as good as Hyman. Well, it's far from the greatest thrill of my life being a ten-year asylum for that man. But I'm concerned about you. Everyone knows you're going to be about as fine an accountant *and* business-man as this firm has seen. I would create a terrific position for you with plenty of room to grow if you ever decide to stay. What I'm trying to get through that thick skull of yours is that if you still plan to emigrate to Israel, I may be able to help you."

Shimshon slid the ashtray along the coffee table's surface.

Sam went over to the windows and looked down at Broadway. "Your work impresses me enough to stake you if you want to start a firm in Israel."

"Did you take charity when you started out?" Shimshon said. "I can never repay you for the visa you guaranteed, but I don't need you to be the Jewish Agency anymore."

"I'm not offering you charity." Sam sat in his desk chair, lifted a paperweight, and began leafing through the documents underneath. "The deal is that in exchange for half the firm's stock, I secure the money to get you off the ground and meet payroll. I also can supply the clients." Sam held up a few documents. "See these? Some clients of mine, diamond dealers in particular, are opening offices in Israel. They need accountants and I need an affiliate I can trust. That makes you a good investment."

Shimshon smiled. "When I've learned enough, I may just take you up on that offer."

"And what will you do about Hyman?"

Shimshon walked across the rug and stood beside Sam's desk. "I plan to take him with me."

"That's what I figured you thought." Sam pointed to the chair in front of his desk. "Sit down. I'll do everything I can to help you get Hyman to move. But I'm telling you. He won't leave this office."

"Oh yeah? Have you watched him lately?" Shimshon said, settling into the chair across from Sam. "He's changed a lot. He talks to Faye every morning, and instead of dropping his worksheets on her desk at night, he hands them to her. 'I hope you have a nice evening, Mrs. Sondheimer,' he says, and bows like a gentleman. Last week she brought him coffee in a mug and two pieces of *tzveibach*. When he returned the empty mug to her, she made sure to tell him that she had baked a whole cake for her boys. Faye and Hyman are lovebirds. Come to think of it, Hyman may be too busy here to go to Israel."

"Fat chance."

"Time will tell, Sam. Time will tell."

"And if it tells wrong, you'll be in Israel and I'll be here picking up the pieces of Hyman Schwartz."

Shimshon seemed annoyed. "Do you want me to treat him like a crystal vase?"

"No. Like the kind of man he is. I've lived with him for over ten years. I've watched him take meticulous care of a new suit for one year and then spend the next nine turning it into shit. Something is very wrong with that man. I wish I shared your confidence. Having been around Hyman longer, I don't." Sam fiddled with an onyx ashtray. "I know you have work to do. Think over my offer."

For a while after Shimshon left the office, Sam sat mulling over what Shimshon had said. Finally, he slammed his fist on the desk, strode straight down the corridor and knocked on the glass outside Hyman's cubicle. "Mr. Schwartz?"

"Yes." Hyman smiled and turned around. "Please come in, Mr. Teitlebaum. Don't wait in the hall."

"Thank you, Mr. Schwartz. How are you?"

"I'm in my office, with interesting work. I'm fine Mr. Teitlebaum." Hyman's smile evaporated; his voice turned serious. "Maybe you have some special reason for asking?"

"I've just been thinking. Every teacher should have lots of students."

"I'm no teacher. You know I made an exception for Shimshon." Hyman looked at Sam suspiciously. "It's not like you to ask for lots of exceptions."

"I've just hired two new men. Nathanson and Karnovsky.

They're very good, but I need a seasoned man to look over their work for a while. I was just sort of hoping you'd change your mind about teaching and supervising and would take them on."

"Only a man who can't do the work becomes a teacher. I sit in my office, I do good work. Why do you want me to waste time with pupils? I have Shimshon. He's more than enough."

Sam pushed himself out of the chair. "Think it over, Mr. Schwartz. Maybe some other time. I'd be very grateful if you thought it over."

Chapter Twenty-one

AT THE NEXT DAY'S LUNCH, Shimshon told Hyman the news: that if Shimshon's work kept up, Sam no longer would require that Abromowitz supervise him.

Hyman became reflective. It seemed like an eternity ago that Shimshon had slouched against the doorjamb and said, "Break bread with *mishpucha*." Hyman had never imagined then that nine months later he would be teaching Shimshon the way a father teaches his son. But if Shimshon stopped needing Abromowitz in June, when would he stop needing Hyman? Hyman stifled sudden tears.

Shimshon prattled on about what a satisfaction Hyman's teaching was. Hyman feigned interest, nodded mechanically and shifted in his chair. He stared at Shimshon's face as if photographing it for memory. He silently begged the clock's hands to accelerate. The moment St. Anne's tolled twelve forty-five, he ended lunch and got back to work.

That afternoon Hyman pressed too hard and broke a pencil point. He almost panicked. Sharpen that point. Sharpen it now. No pencil sits on my desk with its head missing. Hyman worked feverishly and diligently until five thirty. By then, the other cubicles were empty. When he entered the small antechamber in front of the elevator, he was surprised: Shimshon was standing there.

"Would you believe the elevator ran off without me?" Shimshon said. "May I join you on the stairs?"

Hyman shrugged his shoulders. "It's a free country."

Shimshon seemed jittery. He wiped his palms on his slacks as if he expected the stairway door to be stiff and wanted to prevent his fingers from slipping on the metal knob. He thrust his shoulders full-force into the door. It flung open and he stumbled through off balance, his body's full weight ahead of him. He straightened the Star of David, which had been flung onto his shoulder. "It's been a while since I took the stairs," he said sheepishly. "But you told me you prefer them."

Shimshon led the way down. "I guess I'm lucky. By missing the elevator I get to spend extra time with you. Here," he said when they reached the ground floor. "Let me open the way for the world's number-one best teacher." He flung open the fire door.

Hyman stared quizzically at Shimshon for a full ten seconds. "You got the grippe or something?"

Shimshon stepped out of 1225 and walked up Broadway, shoulder-to-shoulder with Hyman. Hyman stopped repeatedly, looked at Shimshon's Star of David and shook his head no; Shimshon smiled as though he had just been asked to say "cheese." Hyman kept walking. Shimshon had never waited for him at the elevator or made nervous, stupid jokes. As they came to Thirty-second Street, they entered the warm light of a late spring sun.

"Please, Mr. Schwartz," Shimshon said. "Let's stop in Greeley Square and talk a while."

"I'll be late getting home."

"It's important, Mr. Schwartz. Please."

Hyman stood on the corner staring at Shimshon for what seemed like a long time. "Just this once," he finally said. Crossing Thirty-second Street, they walked into the park and sat on a bench. "So what do you need to talk about? I know that in July you won't need Abromowitz. Soon the time will come when you don't need me either."

Hyman watched the horde of pigeons battling for the bread crusts a vagrant woman had thrown on the sidewalk. Pigeons swarmed in the late afternoon sun, darted and pecked one another's opalescent necks competing for morsels. The woman carried a rag-filled shopping bag and looked painted. Red lipstick was smeared beyond the borders of her mouth; each cheek was caked with a full moon of orange face powder. "Eat-a Rosie's food," the woman shouted. "Eat-a Mama's food, babies."

The two men were silent. Wheels screeched on Broadway. People hurried to the subway. Hyman watched a mother and a boy no older than three entering the park near Thirty-fourth Street. Red suspenders crossed the back of the boy's clean white shirt and held up his royal blue shorts. Mother and son sat on a bench; smiling, he nuzzled into her side. He climbed down from his bench carefully and crouched to try and pet a pigeon. His bottom almost touched his shoes.

"There's nothing really to talk about," Hyman said. "Facts are facts. Students grow up and move on. That's life."

The little boy across the way held out his hands and ran toward a pigeon. It squawked and flew toward the Stanford Hotel. The boy ran after another, then a third. Suddenly the entire flock flushed and flew away. The boy returned to his mother, sad-faced. "Why no play?"

"You scared them, Chris." The mother laughed.

The painted lady rushed toward the boy wagging her finger. "Get-a the hell outa here," she screeched, holding up her shopping bag. "I'm-a gonna hit you. Superman said to a-stop hurting my babies!"

The boy disintegrated. His mother swept her bawling son into her arms, stared at the painted woman and put civility and understatement aside. "Get lost!" Her voice threatened violence; the painted woman spit on the ground, glared at the mother and walked away. The mother stroked her son's hair and carried him toward Thirty-fourth Street. "Don't cry, sweetie. That lady's sick." The mother started singing.

"Get your coat, put on your hat. Leave your worries on the doorstep." She turned as if waltzing with her son. The boy stopped bawling and put his finger in his mouth.

Mothers and sons. Did Rachel's song embrace David as they walked to the end?

"You know I'm planning to go to Israel, Mr. Schwartz. What worries me is that I may have to move alone."

"So find yourself a nice girl to take along." Hyman saw the mother carrying her son out of Greeley Square. Now the boy was smiling and laughing as his mother tickled his underarm. If only I had realized what was coming a few years earlier. Rachel and I could have carried David away from the lunatics. "Find yourself a nice girl."

"I'll find a wife in Israel. But I won't find a teacher like you anywhere."

"Look and you'll find. You'll probably find a teacher better than me. But don't worry yourself. Even after you stop with Abromowitz, I'll keep teaching you until you're ready to leave."

"What really worries me, Mr. Schwartz, is that when I move to Israel, you won't move with me."

"Move with you? What are you, nuts? Of course I won't move with you. I struggled ten years to get things that came easy to you. I've built a life for myself here. Maybe for a young man it's different, but it's hard for an old man to learn what to do with his life. I learned and I know and I'm good at it. Leaving is hard for everyone. But when a man goes out on his own, he doesn't take his teacher along."

"You're my friend. I want you to come with me."

"My job is to teach you. No use to talk about moving," Hyman said and stood up. "New York's my home now. The weekend's here and for the time being you're not ready to leave. We both have to get home."

Hyman left and did not look back. He walked uptown absorbed in thought. He's got to be crazy. Me move? I worked ten years to learn English. I can't move to a place whose language I don't speak. I spent ten years trying to forget what I lost; I don't want to live in a country where every corner reminds me.

Hyman ate dinner at the Automat, registering only dimly the noises of dropped silver and the clip-clop of feet ascending the staircase to the second level. *How stupid can a young boy be? I'm not his friend. I'm old enough to be his father. And like Papa taught me, you don't take your father along when you leave home.*

After dinner Hyman walked into the park through the Children's Gate. *Shimshon wants me to start again in a country of living corpses. He's nuts.* As Hyman passed Roth's statue of a bear, dancing to the tune played by frogs singing and playing ukuleles at his feet, he suddenly felt swept back in time and was strolling Rava's paths. *Is that you, Papa, or is it the mountain cedars whispering, "So what's our name? Even Adam knew what to call us. Shouldn't you?"*

A boy ran out of Central Park's dairy, brushed past Hyman and ran to the carousel's fiery horses. Time and locale shifted. *Is that you, David? Is this Bradalska Park?* A speckled caterpillar descended on a gossamer thread toward a footpath near Hecksher Playground. Hyman crouched beside it. *David? Are you waiting for me around the next corner?* He stood and held aloft a shivering hand. "It's King David's sword, Papa. King David's Sword."

The sunset had painted low western clouds with blazing brushstrokes. Although nighttime danger would soon prowl the paths, Hyman was not ready to be home. He needed a crowd to be lost in. Who knows? Maybe he would get lucky and bump into Shimshon so he could tell him over again that his suggestion was ridiculous. *I'm almost fifty. I know you for less than a year. I've worked more than ten times that long to get my place at the firm and to know what to do from one day to the next. You expect me to leave all that?*

The springtime air was warm and soothing. Stars blossomed in the royal blue sky. When Hyman reached Forty-fifth Street and turned east, he was facing the huge,

144

undulating awning above the Lyceum Theater and the very same doorman in a maroon uniform he had seen last Yom Kippur Eve. I'm used to these streets now, Shimshon. Since I started answering your questions, I don't see camp guards anymore. When I hear sirens, I don't jump in alleys to escape Gestapo coming to round me up. Will the shadows come back when you leave?

Since theatergoers had already disappeared into their shows, the crowd Hyman walked amidst was thin. He passed a young woman in a long, Poodle skirt. He edged over to one side watching as she held her boyfriend by his biceps, raised herself on her toes, and kissed his lips. Laughing, she ran down the street pulling the young man after her.

A woman's lips once kissed mine, Hyman thought. But a fifty-year-old's days as a lover ended long ago. Now it's Shimshon's turn. He shouldn't risk it by even considering dragging along an old man.

Hyman wandered the theater district, past derelicts and drifters, past a pimp with a ruby sparkling in his black ear, past hawkers, hookers, hustlers, newspaper boys, a gentleman twirling a cane and his lady marveling at his skill. He passed assorted beggars, cripples, tarts, and all those forms of life, high and low, that gave Times Square and the theater district its distinctive flavor.

At ten fifteen he walked pensively through the Excelsior's lobby and up the staircase. Israel's the other side of the moon, he thought. Look how much I've got here. He bolted his door, flipped on the light, and sat on his bed. Troubled and exhausted, he surveyed the bare walls, the paint chipping off the vertical bars at the foot of his bed. Suddenly, he was confronting himself. If Shimshon Tisza was crazy, so am I, to cling to empty walls and a sink I'll never use because on Yom Kippur Eve I pissed in it. Even Hyman's bedframe testified to his madness; its white metal bars looked more suited to a mental institution than to a home.

What kind of man chooses to live like this? God gave me shit, but I gave myself this room. Hyman started to get excited. Maybe I should move. It's high time I was good to myself. I'll go to Israel. Shimshon and I will start our own office, with accountants, bookkeepers and secretaries running here and there with Schwartz and Tisza business.

Hyman was energized. Let Shimshon get married. I'll be the Papa who's thrilled to give him away. And every Sabbath I'll visit him and his wife and eventually the grandchildren as well. Why not? We'll run a firm so good that God Himself will bow down, awed by how flawlessly we keep books. Why not? It's high time Shimshon and I made a better life for ourselves. To hell with God.

But then his viewpoint changed; the angle shifted. Who are you kidding, Hyman Schwartz? You worked ten years to be able to get through a day without going totally mad. Now that you know how to survive, you're going to become a greenhorn again just because a stranger tells you to follow his rainbow? After the roads you've traveled and all you've seen, you still believe in rainbows and pots of gold? Who are you kidding? You can't oppose His will. If God wanted a better life for you, He would have given you one. Forget this *narishkeit* and go to sleep. You know who the Boss is.

Chapter Twenty-two

WHEN HYMAN AWOKE, sunlight was peering under the windowshade. He stretched, rubbed the slumber out of his eyes, brushed his thin hair with his hands and stumbled to his armchair. What do I have here? No pictures on the walls, no silver in a breakfront, no fruit in a bowl or candles on the dining room table. Dining room table? I haven't got a dining room, kitchen, or even toilet of my own. When I first saw this room I saw a palace filled with every luxury a man could ever want. Hyman stroked the chair's worn velvet arms. Now if Shimshon came to visit, I don't even have a second chair to offer him.

Hyman went to the shower room, shaking his head disapprovingly all the way down the hall. He undressed and tried to adjust the water. But no matter how delicately he turned the knobs, he could not get the water to a comfortable temperature. Nothing seemed right today. So Hyman stepped into water too cold for his tastes, washed himself quickly and went back to his room disgruntled.

He dressed, spun up his windowshade and stared at Abelman's carcass. The red had flaked away; an outline was all that remained. Mr. Abelman hasn't repainted his sign in ten years, Hyman thought. Soon you won't even be able to tell that it's meat. It and me, we're both getting old and no one's looking out for either of us. Me? For over ten years I've run away from my pictures. What have I done? No past, no present, no future. A man might as well be dead.

Hyman got the envelope down from the upper shelf of his closet, sat back in his chair and unlaced the closure. The photographs curled forward. Hyman took deep breaths, as if through long slow breathing he could tame his terror. He grasped one picture—it was Rachel on their wedding day—half expecting its molecules to shimmer and her white dress to swirl the way it had when they danced that dreamy night. He sat quietly listening for the swish of the lace.

But nothing remotely pleasurable happened. Rather, dread assaulted him. It was as if bony fingers emerged from those pictures, closed around Hyman's neck and started choking him. Unable to catch his breath, he stood abruptly; the envelope fell off his lap. In panic, as he looked for a way to escape, he saw Papa so clearly that Hyman felt his father actually was in the room with him. He heard Papa's soft voice: "Is it finally getting through, Hyman? Last time we spoke you said you understood how I felt when I put you on the train to Warsaw. Understanding is only with the head. To really comprehend, your heart has to know how mine was breaking on the worst day of my life."

Papa. Shimshon wants me to move with him. When Rachel and I married, you talked about moving to Warsaw some day.

"But I never did. When a couple marries, the wife needs her husband to herself. So I had to leave you there alone even though I missed you and her and, later, David every day. Do you know how hard it was for me to see my grandson only every six months? But letting you build your own life wasn't my only reason. I had a business in Rava and a wife who was happy only when she lived near the rebbe."

What should I do Papa? If Shimshon didn't really want me to move with him, he never would have asked.

Papa looked right at him. "For religious Jews 'should' is easy. You eat kosher and you stay away from pork. But your question is about what you want."

The warm, spring breeze filtering through the window comforted Hyman. The soft, clean air caressed his cheeks and closed his eyes. He could smell her in the room. He could feel her arms closing around him and knew what he wanted. He remembered drawing her close. She was so willing to come nearer to him, to stroke his face gently and press her body into his. Her embrace was thrilling, her kisses were divine, her breasts were soft and, when the time finally came and he entered, her invitation was wet, frictionless and enthusiastic. Hyman inhaled, recalling her smile, clasp and moans when they loved, feeling her hugging him intensely, inhaling their lovemaking's tart, musky fragrance.

"That's the question now, son. What do you want?"

Hyman ran his right hand sensuously down his left arm, slowly over his fingers and onto the cold cotton bedspread. Tears filled his eyes. Look what love's become.

He needed to get away from his desires and out of this room. The walls assaulted him with loneliness. Metal slats on his bed accused him of lunacy. He feared that his photographs would drive him mad; even their curled edges roused his deepest dread. Each one beseeched, "Do not forsake us," and swore that the hugs and love that had warmed him in his Warsaw apartment, the aromas that had greeted him every Sabbath eve, that even David and Rachel themselves could be recaptured simply by untying a shoestring.

Since Kol Nidre night, so much had come clearer to Hyman. He had to admit that when he had accepted a place in *Leviathan*'s hold, his mind knew that David and Rachel might never come back. But his heart had circumvented facts and gone into hiding. When no cable had yet arrived on the first anniversary of his coming to the firm, he had stayed up all night ensconced deep in the corner of an emotional cave. That night, he could just barely find his heart, discern his sorrow and know why he was weeping.

So he used the technique he had first developed in Buna. He had started moving numbers through his head. Moving inward was his only way to exile every last vestige of feeling and to live in suspended animation in this New World. That method had worked flawlessly until Hyman had stood up straight and accused God outright. Then, in his rage, his heart had been freed from its crypt. And since that evening, in every private moment and as he lay in bed ruminating, he remembered how her body felt and wished he could forget.

He had tried to retreat into numbers again. And he knew that his retreat might have succeeded if Shimshon had not persisted and provoked him to violence. If. If my aunt had balls she'd be my uncle. Shimshon had succeeded, and had afflicted him with a detached man's ultimate enemy, the one that makes you lose your entire sense of cool mathematical judgment, the one hope that seduces you to believe that the future is open and that anything is possible. Shimshon had become his friend.

Hyman retied the manila envelope, put it in the closet and hurried to the subway. More than thirteen years had passed since his family had been marched away. Thirteen years of longing, thirteen years of lonely commitment, thirteen years of refusing to say good-bye and to let them die and disappear in the peace the stupid ones called rest. I buried my pictures so we'd have good memories to come home to. Now Shimshon says I should start again even though David, Rachel and I will never be a "we" again. Doesn't he know that time doesn't heal? It hardly even dulls.

Hyman rushed down the subway stairs, through the turnstile and into the green train waiting on the platform. Walking down the aisle, he looked for a seat whose woven wicker was intact. But many had lacquer chipped off and splinters protruding from their surface. He avoided seats that could accidentally rip his clothing. Ten years had passed since he had begun tearing his clothes. He would never let the boss know, but the tears were neither accidental nor signs of wear. No. He recalled the first lapel he had torn ten years earlier when he desperately needed to let everyone know that if you once had a woman who spun you in the heavens with each embrace, you don't just forget and start over again.

The train roared through the black subway tunnel; solitary incandescent bulbs flashed past and evaporated in ghostly trails. Just like love, Hyman thought. A burst of light that leaves only darkness behind. In February, twenty-one years will have passed since I pledged myself. And now Shimshon wants me to give up my dream.

In Brooklyn, the train rolled into sunlight. Although he was still miles away, Hyman thought he could already hear the surf roaring and smell the brine spewing in the air.

He passed stop after stop. Finally, the train pulled into the Brighton Beach station. Hyman got off and crossed the wide boardwalk. He stared past the Atlantic's western shore and bubbling surf, past waves, past a rust-orange fishing boat bobbing near the horizon. A gentle ocean breeze caressed his face and whispered a lullaby of waves crashing on the sandy shore.

He sat on a bench, closed his eyes and felt the breeze brush his cheeks. "Why does an ocean separate us, Rachel?" Hyman murmured. "Soon it will be our twenty-first anniversary. To me, our wedding night could have been yesterday. Remember the *chupah?* Even though you knew that when a bride waits under it she's supposed to look straight ahead, you disobeyed. When I was five feet away, your white lace veil trembled as you turned toward me. There, under the *chupah,* before the wedding, with God and everyone in both our families watching, you looked right into my eyes and smiled. That smile may be twenty-one years old, but for me it shines more brightly than any star ever could. When I remember that smile I feel like my heart will explode into fragments and that tears will run down my face until time ends.

"Rachel. When I agreed to teach Shimshon, I said that I'd need your strength. Maybe I deceived you."

Hyman's head hung down. "I didn't tell you that now I also say hello to Mrs. Sondheimer, eat her cakes and listen to stories about her boys." Hyman turned back to the ocean. "That's what I have to ask. Does eating her cakes and becoming interested in her mean I can't sleep with you in the hereafter?"

A wave crashed on the shore. "Don't laugh. If there's no God and no hereafter, your answer doesn't matter. But if there is, will you never forgive me for holding another? Will you say that since I ate another woman's food, in the hereafter I have to stay an ocean apart from you? I can't do that, Rachel. It killed me once. Don't you understand? Where are you? Answer me!" Hyman screamed. Peaks of incoming waves ignited in the midday sun, rose in flaming glory and collapsed, churning sunlight with foam and spreading it on the shore like diamonds strewn on wet sand. Waters receded, leaving behind a wash of foam and a flat shoreline that shimmered like ground glass.

Hyman walked the boardwalk, following the gray, weathered grain of the wooden planks. That's my life. I spent eleven years waiting for your cable, sweetheart. I'll wait another thousand if that's what you say I have to do to lure you back. But now I see color in Shimshon's food. And Rachel, now he doesn't show off his smile. Now he shows off what a fine accountant he's become. But it's more than just him. Now when I taste Mrs. Sondheimer's food I hear music again.

Hyman left the boardwalk and thought: Once the question was whether to teach a boy with a big mouth and a number on his arm. Now the question's more complicated. I've got a room and a job. I've learned English and taught myself how to get around the city. I'm comfortable here. Should I leave? Should I stay? Should I be what I am or start over again?

Hyman rode home, his head in his hands, his eyes fixed on the heel-scuffed floor. The question is what do I want? What's right for Shimshon? What's right for me?

That night Hyman's sleep was restless. The next morning he calculated parts of the nine scale: 3 times 90 equals 270, 3 times 99 equals 297, which is obvious since it's 3 less than 100 times 3. Simple. But a man who didn't gradually work up from the beginning would overlook how simple 99 times 333 is, 32,967—333 less than 100 times 333. And he would faint if he saw 211 times 333. But it's easy too: 70,263. You just have to break the problem into its parts. Multiply 211 by 1,000, which is 3 times 333, plus 1. Subtract 211 and divide by 3. That division is simple. It's not much harder if you do 200 times 333, plus 11 times 333. Tricks. That's all counting fast is. Tricks your mind plays faster the more you practice.

But today numbers did not fence in Hyman's imagination. He thought he heard Shimshon laugh; he smelled Faye Sondheimer's cakes. He knew that if he didn't stop feeling he would go out of his mind. At five he went to Central Park, hooked his thumbs behind him and walked in the shade of magnolia and oak leaves, headed toward the lake. The weeping willows hanging over Bethesda Fountain reminded him of what the religious part of his Rava education taught him happened to Jews who let themselves feel: "By the waters of Babylon, there we sat down and wept when we remembered Zion. On the willows there we hung our lyres. For there our captors required of us songs, and our tormentors, mirth, saying, 'Sing us one of the songs of Zion!' "

Stooped, Hyman headed up the West Drive. He loathed happy people, stupid aliens like the boy buying a Good Humor bar and the old couple holding hands. Where did you spend the war, old man? You're old and bent enough to know the truth. Tomorrow your woman will turn to ashes.

When the sky darkened at dusk, Hyman stomped downtown. He read incandescent headlines racing around the Times Building: EISENHOWER . . . NASSER . . . DULLES . . . EDEN . . . MOLLET . . . SECURITY COUNCIL . . . SUEZ. I spent years learning to read English. Why leave now? In early evening, Hyman wandered the theater district until the streets overflowed with men and women who felt uplifted by New York theater. Then he had to leave because a subspecies he could not understand had taken over the city's streets.

Hyman was overjoyed when Monday dawned. He came to work early because he would be too embarrassed to run into Mrs. Sondheimer. Luckily, Sam came before eight and let him in. Hyman concentrated on worksheets all morning. When Shimshon came to the doorway at noon, Hyman was immersed in calculations. But he turned to glance at the red curls and blue eyes in the doorway, then went back to the Victor and kept working. He knew that he ought to recognize the voice that said, "Are you all right?" and should feel appreciative for food this man was setting out. But he felt detached as he watched pears and plums settle on his desk. He scratched his head vigorously.

"What did you decide?" Shimshon said.

Now Hyman recalled why he felt detached. He took out the sandwiches and pickles. There's only one thing to do, he thought. You can't risk spending the hereafter alone. Change the subject. Talk about something else, anything else. "I decided that you don't have enough patience to learn to count fast in your head." Numbers. Talk numbers.

Shimshon laughed. "A challenge from the maestro. What makes you think that the man who vanquished blackhearted Victor himself doesn't have the patience to learn to count fast?"

"You really believe you can do it?"

Shimshon put his elbows on Hyman's desk. "I really believe you're evading the important question, which is whether you'll be in Israel to teach me."

"No. What's important now is making sure your work is so meticulous that the boss never regrets letting you work on your own." Hyman handed a ledger book to Shimshon. "For the next month, you'll review my work, and I'm going to check every bit of yours. Let's eat fast. We have lots to do."

"But we have to talk about Israel."

"Israel can wait." Hyman looked about furtively and whispered. "After your first two weeks of working alone, Mr. Teitlebaum may tell you to work with Abromowitz again. Then neither of us will be going to Israel."

"But . . ."

"No buts. There's nothing to talk about."

All June long, whenever Shimshon brought up Israel, Hyman changed the subject. Did you make sure your debits and credits match? I know I warned you a hundred times. But if you're going to work on your own, I have to warn you the hundred and first . . .

They reviewed each other's work. Hyman made no mistakes; Shimshon's were trivial. But Hyman persevered, repeating old lessons, maxims and homilies until Shimshon wanted to return Hyman's eight-month-old punch.

Chapter Twenty-three

HOT WEATHER seized the city in early summer and held it tightly. On the morning of June 28, Sam walked into his office, threw his seersucker jacket on a chair, loosened his tie and lay down on the couch. Shimshon knocked on his door, came in and slumped in the armchair opposite Sam.

"Do you believe this weather?" Sam said. "It's not July yet, and it feels like mid-August. So what do you say about my proposition?"

"*Schwartz*, Tisza, and Teitlebaum."

"Call it whatever you want. But names won't change facts."

"So why did Hyman hint that he might move?"

Sam sat up. "Cut it out! He didn't really say he would go."

"On the Friday before Memorial Day he said that since I wasn't ready to leave, he didn't have to rush his decision."

Sam leaned toward Shimshon. "Decision?"

"Yeah. Hyman really did hint he'd think about moving. Now I'm worried. At the end of May, I was sure I'd gotten through. But by June first all Hyman would do is review old lessons."

"That means you got through."

"He hasn't fallen apart. But he scratches himself and tears off the scabs like he doesn't want them to heal."

Sam walked to the open window and looked down. Cabs

156

were honking. Two men, each with a bale of furs slung over his shoulder, were arguing on the corner of Thirtieth Street. Nearby, a fire engine's siren wailed. "Do you believe this city? It's not even the Fourth of July and it's already a madhouse. But at least in the good old U.S. of A. you don't have to worry about malaria and fedayeen. Stay here, Shimshon. I'll teach you about the Dodgers and baseball. And we'll build this firm into a world-class outfit."

"I'm headed east. But Hyman's my friend. Something terrible could happen to him if he stays."

"Something terrible happened to him long before you arrived."

"You care about a man, Sam, think he's interested in living. Then he acts like all he wants to be is dead."

Sam sat down again. "I never could figure Hyman out. A few months after he came here he started picking at himself. It was terrible to watch. So when he started tearing clothes instead, I was relieved."

"He tears his clothes on purpose?"

"A meticulous man has to work to look like him. For his first five months here, Hyman's clothes looked like they had just come off the rack. The day Sharp left, Hyman began destroying them. I take that personally. It's like he checks me out regularly, looks at me as if he's saying, 'You really like yourself, don't you? Let's see how you perform on a simple test to see whether you're a man of your word, whether you meant it when you said you didn't care how I dress.' Maybe I'm nuts, but I think there's a method to his madness. I sense it every day. I just wish he'd realize that testing me isn't worth wasting his life on."

Shimshon paced the rug, and muttered "Damn" a few times.

"Sorry to scare you," Sam said. "But any man you deal with has a history. We're not all the same except for the fact that we all make mistakes." He noticed Shimshon's frustration deepening. "Hey, listen. We all do stupid things. Hyman locks himself in a cubicle trying to settle a universal score. And I played a game pushing you to get Hyman to teach you. Sometimes I wish I hadn't. But you have a life of your own. You can't become Hyman's guardian or hostage."

"What should I do?"

"You've already done more than I thought was possible. Since Hyman started teaching you, he talks to me, even says good morning to the other accountants. Let's hope that he has some good sense left. But in regard to accounting, you need to learn administration. Welcome to Teitlebaum U. Next month I start teaching you how to run a firm." Sam scratched his cheek. "I know ignoring this situation won't stop Hyman from going nuts. If he does, I'll find him the best psychiatrist in town. You may not be ready to leave just yet. But you're not far away. I know it. You know it. I can assure you that Hyman Schwartz knows it too."

Shimshon pounded the desk with his fist. "Damn!"

"Breaking your fingers won't help. But I never imagined Hyman would even agree to *think* about moving. Neither of us has a crystal ball. So go back to work and let's hope."

Chapter Twenty-four

JULY SECOND was a landmark. Late that afternoon, rather than showing his work to Abromowitz, Shimshon went to Sam's office and began learning how to solicit business, allocate work, select a lawyer and satisfy clients.

With Shimshon promoted, Hyman knew it was ridiculous to insist that out of deep concern for Shimshon's well-being he had to check each of his computations, which unfortunately left no time for discussions. Pens, ledgers and Victor were ancient history. The only discipline left to teach was the one nearest his heart, the last defense to obfuscate feeling, the art he called "counting in your head."

At every lunch for the first two weeks of July Hyman spoke with mounting desperation about how disciplining the human mind to do mathematics was the ultimate human achievement, the creation of a world whose perfection made one forget the absurdity of God's. He insisted fervently that minor personal details like where one lived were maggots compared to the Monarch-butterfly elegance of arithmetic. "Counting fast in your head takes years of practice," Hyman said in the third week of July, his enthusiasm manic. "Perseverance separates the men from the boys. No matter who discourages him, no matter who tells him that there's just so far he can go with numbers, a real man forges ahead. Counting in my head is the most important lesson in my life."

159

Hyman counted the floor's linoleum squares in his mind as his fingers picked mindlessly at his arm.

"Will you stop that," Shimshon said.

"It's just a nervous habit. I know an excellent trick, Shimshon. Have you ever learned the rules of elevens?"

"I don't know."

Hyman stopped picking at his arm.

Relieved, Shimshon said, "Tell it to me."

"You'll probably recognize it when I tell you. Smart schoolchildren pick up its simple form. The rule is so beautiful that it holds for multiplying *any* two-digit number by eleven. Let's say, just for example, that you want to multiply forty-four by eleven. You spread the multiplicand's digits apart, four/empty space/four, add the two digits together, four plus four makes eight, put that sum between the spread digits and you have your answer: four-eight-four. Eleven times twenty-seven makes two-nine-seven. Isn't that wonderful?"

Amused, Shimshon nodded. "Of course I know that. But what do you do when the two digits add up to more than nine?"

"Now that's the part that schoolboys stumble over." Hyman leaned across the desk, tapping his fingers on the glass top to emphasize points. "Whenever the sum of the digits exceeds nine, add the first digit of the sum, always a one, to the hundreds column, and put the second digit in the middle. Eleven times sixty-six makes seven hundred twenty-six. If you already have a nine in the hundreds column, make it a ten and put the one in the thousands column. Eleven times ninety-eight makes ten-seven-eight, because when you add the one from the seventeen—nine plus eight makes seventeen, right?—to the nine in the hundreds column, you get a ten. When you get better at it, I'll teach you how to apply the rule to three-digit numbers. Make no mistake. A trick like that moves you a lot faster. And I've got a lot more tricks where that one came from." Hyman simpered.

"I'm sure you do."

Sensing sarcasm, Hyman again began to scratch. A flash of pain drove him inward, forcing him to grapple with a disturbance he could no longer suppress. "We don't talk like we used to, do we?"

Shimshon nodded.

"I wish I could talk the easy way you do." Hyman put his elbows on his knees, his head in his hands, and stared at the floor. "I don't know what to do."

"Help build a new world!"

"Don't sell me dreams about changing the world. I've been around long enough to know how hard a man struggles just to change his smallest habit."

"At least try. Israel wants you."

Hyman picked a shred of white paper off the floor, dropped it and watched it float into the trash can. "That's easy to say when you're young, with hope and a whole life ahead of you. The world looks different to an old man."

"Mr. Schwartz. I want you to be my partner. We could call our firm Schwartz, Tisza, and Teitlebaum."

"Why Teitlebaum? Is Mr. Teitlebaum moving?"

"Sam's a New Yorker through and through. But he wants to invest his money in an Israeli firm. He's been teaching me management. Come to Israel. Forty-nine is still young."

"Counting the number of years a man's lived is the most trivial way to measure his age. In some ways I feel like I've had over eighty years' experience. Give me time." Hyman looked directly at Shimshon, his eyes moist. "You'll be gone in less than six months."

"And you?"

"If I knew where I'd be in six months, I'd tell you." Then Hyman thought words he felt too shy to say out loud. No matter what I decide, no matter what happens after you go, I'll always *kvell* about how well I've taught you and how well you've learned. But what's left to teach? You won't spend ten years learning to count fast in your head. Someday soon you'll have a wife, a son and a life of your own. "I don't ever want you to feel forced to be here. You'd be smart to eat lunch with Mr. Teitlebaum. Now he's the one with something to teach."

"Don't." Shimshon put his hand on Hyman's.

"Almost a year, Shimshon. You really learned well. Some people would call us friends."

Shimshon squeezed Hyman's hand gently. "We've been friends for a long time. I eat lunch with you because I like to. I'd even like to eat lunch with you in Israel. If we stop eating lunches together, it's your decision."

"Don't say that." Hyman pulled away his hand and began to scratch it. "You can't read the future. What makes you so sure that when you have a family and friends of a family, you'll still want to eat lunch with me?"

"I'm not positive what will happen this afternoon. But my friendships aren't transient."

"Just don't tell me that you know what will happen the day after tomorrow."

"Buy insurance. Make a few friends in addition to me."

"Don't be ridiculous. I already know everyone here." Calmed by thinking of how well Shimshon had learned, Hyman stopped scratching himself. "You know it's very stuffy in here lately. Maybe you'll agree with an idea I've been considering. Let's eat in Greeley Square tomorrow."

"Are you serious?"

"Is there something wrong with Greeley?"

Shimshon had doubted he was actually hearing Hyman invite him to eat in Greeley Square. Sam said that Hyman would never leave the firm. Well if Hyman was so damned inflexible, why was he proposing that they leave Teitlebaum & Sharfenstein, walk two blocks uptown, cross Thirty-second Street and eat lunch in Greeley Square? Because he was too hot in the office? Don't be ridiculous. He could loosen his tie or stop wearing an undershirt. "You have a deal. Tomorrow in Greeley Square." Shimshon winked and said, "And maybe next year in Jerusalem."

Chapter Twenty-five

FROM THEN UNTIL MID-AUGUST, Hyman picked up Shimshon at lunchtime and walked with him to the same Greeley Square bench. They constantly had to shoo away pigeons who fluttered around their hands, assuming that bread in Greeley Square was a proffered invitation. Cars honked. Noontime shoppers shuttled through Macy's doors. Lunchgoers hurried to air-conditioned restaurants and coffee shops.

One sunny day early in August, just after Hyman shooed away a pigeon that had fluttered near his head and tried to land on his shoulder, Shimshon said. "What's with you and Faye?"

"Nothing!"

"A piece of coffee cake here, a slice of *boimikuchen* there. Talk about her boys today," Shimshon winked, "and before you know it you'll be at her place for dinner."

"You're crazy." With his fingernail, Hyman picked at his pants' stitchwork. I had one wife and we're forever. "Mrs. Sondheimer is nice to me, so I say hello. What's wrong with that?"

"Then you have no reason to stay in New York. I'll start planning. We wouldn't have to scrounge around for money if we were partners with Sam."

"I don't want him," Hyman blurted out. He furrowed his brow and spoke slowly. "I don't know. How can I know about Mr. Teitlebaum before I decide about myself? You've got a good position here. Why leave?"

"In public I'd say, 'Because I'm proud to be a descendant of King David!' " Shimshon picked up a pebble and rolled it between his fingers. "But anyone who's been where we were can't be all that proud. We had to do too many ugly things just to stay alive."

Shimshon skittered the pebble across the asphalt. "I don't ever want there to be any more walking dead," he went on. "Until Hitler arrived, my father hardly knew he was Jewish. We didn't even go to synagogue on Yom Kippur. After all, we were more assimilated than Neologs, who were to Hungary what reformed Jews were to Germany. My family were atheists. To me there's as much a God as there is a man in the moon. But my father refused to change religions even though he knew it would be to his business advantage. If you don't believe in the Jewish God, why pray to a Jewish boy? Half of my relatives were Catholic."

"You had Catholic relatives?"

"Don't look so surprised, Mr. Schwartz. Do you believe there were Jews and Aryans and their blood never mixed? That's what our great Premier Imrédy believed. He was a devout Catholic who became such a good Nazi that he sponsored the 'Second anti-Jewish Law' which said that one single drop of Jewish blood was enough to infect a man's character and to make him unpatriotic. A little while later, our regent, Admiral Horthy, summoned Imrédy into his office and showed him an incontrovertible document proving that one of Imrédy's great-grandmothers was Jewish. Imrédy fainted right on the spot. When they revived him, he resigned. But one-eighth was not too much for Hitler. After all, every family makes mistakes. Imrédy went on to be a great Nazi. Then times changed again. After the war, the People's Court executed Imrédy for being a Nazi collaborator.

"Having a lot more than one-eighth Jewish blood was dangerous. I had a distant cousin in Germany who converted just before the First World War, a publisher named Levy. Between the wars they called him 'the Catholic Levy.' He went to church faithfully, until Hitler sent him to the gas."

"I thought you go to synagogue."

"Only with Sam. Sam goes to synagogue to talk to God. I go to talk to Sam."

"So why Israel?"

"My family spoke German at home. After the First World War, when the Austro-Hungarian Empire collapsed, they began to speak more Hungarian at home and became more nationalistic. But my father still said that Germany had the right idea. They were the ones who were good to Jews. Until Hitler became chancellor, the Germans let Jews live in peace and let them prosper. A German Jew was a German first and a Jew second.

"Even when Hungary became Hitler's ally under Horthy, my father felt we would be safe. And Horthy and even Bárdossy, our really anti-Semitic prime minister, actually kept Budapest's Jews away from the camps until the Germans occupied us in 1944 and made Szálasi their puppet premier. He was leader of the Arrow Cross Party, the most vicious anti-Semitic bunch in Hungary.

"When stories about ghettos and the camps began to filter down from Nagykanizsa and Transylvania to Budapest in 1944, my father insisted they had to be paranoid lies. 'The Germans are not the Poles,' he would say. 'They would never go *that* far.' But he did take the precaution, when the Germans came, of getting false papers for my mother and sending her to live with a peasant woman in the country. That's how she survived. We were supposed to join her a few weeks later but they wouldn't let us go. So we ended up in Auschwitz.

"After the war, one government was tolerant to Jews, the next encouraged pogroms. Can you believe it? In 1946, we had pogroms in Kunmadaras and Miskolc. Only a few Jews were killed, but they were real, old-fashioned pogroms. Then the Communists came. They were mainly Jews and declared us antifascists. So we were treated well. But then they changed their minds again, needed some Jews for their show trials, decided we were probably Zionists and blamed us for Hungary's economic problems.

"The others in my family who are alive, even the uncle who bought my exit visa, still say they're Hungarians till the end and that the bad times will be over soon. The Catholic ones think I'm crazy to stay a Jew and the Jews think I'm crazy to go to Israel. But I've seen enough. My future is going to be in Jewish hands."

"I'm confused. I thought you were a Zionist."

"Now I'm a Zionist. I was raised a Hungarian chauvinist and an atheist."

"Would you move to Israel if you never planned to have a family?"

"Why talk about ifs? We need to replenish what we lost."

"But what you imagine, Shimshon, stops you from seeing how important a room I'm used to and a job I'm good at are to me. Please try to put yourself in my shoes. When most of your possibilities passed long ago, when you don't believe in rainbows and pots of gold, to have a routine that gets you through every day without any pain and somebody who considers your work valuable becomes very important." Hyman pulled at a hair on his arm until his loose skin tented like a teepee. "An old man has to work hard just to keep his head on straight."

"Stop picking at yourself. It drives me crazy."

"Don't you see? Sometimes picking at yourself is the only way to remind yourself who you are." Hyman let go of the skin tent, which slowly flattened back into place. "I know you want an answer. Of all people, you deserve to get what you want from me. Since I came to New York, you're the only person I've eaten with. So I keep telling myself I should go to Israel. But for me, going to any new place may be wrong. And sometimes I worry my going would be even worse for you."

"What do you mean?"

Hyman stuffed their trash into the Gristede's bag and dropped it in a nearby rubbish can. He took a deep breath and sighed. "A young man in a new place needs a clean start. No old laundry. Like Papa said, 'I'm yesterday. You have to be tomorrow.' "

166

Chapter Twenty-six

DURING THE LAST WEEKS of August and through early September, Shimshon tried to persuade Hyman that all Jews ought to emigrate. "In Israel, no Jew walks around scared."

"Except about whether his throat will be slit."

Although Hyman had snappy answers to every argument, Shimshon was not deterred. He attacked Hyman's belief that a Jewish man needed a son. "Maybe in the shtetl, a Jewish man needed a son. But now *Am Yisroel Chai*, the nation of Israel is something larger than any one man's family ever could be."

Hyman really did listen to Shimshon's arguments. Although he understood words like *living, dying* and *country*, he disagreed with the idea that a nation could replace flesh and blood. "Wait until you have a family. Then you'd trade all your big ideas to buy your son one warm overcoat. Then you'll understand why Jewish men with sons think small."

Hyman asked Rachel and Papa what to do. But they offered no advice. He was convinced that Shimshon was deluding himself: when Shimshon found a wife and built a life of his own, he would suggest that Hyman join a club and look for other friends. Where will I be then? Hyman thought. Far from my room and the job I know. I'll be locked in a partnership that will tempt me to cripple him. Every time he took a step that didn't include me, I'd feel terrible and he'd feel guilty, then I'd feel guilty for making him feel terrible. I know from experience how hard leaving a papa behind can be. But a man starting his own life has to do it.

In early September, just a few days after Labor Day, Teitlebaum & Sharfenstein closed for the two-day Jewish New Year. When the office reopened, Hyman asked Faye whether she couldn't perhaps, if it wasn't too much trouble of course, arrange an appointment with Sam.

"You're too important for perhapses and maybes. Walk right in, Mr. Schwartz. And by the way, I have some *ruggelach* left over from the holiday. I'll bring them after your meeting."

"You shouldn't have," Hyman said. He paused for a moment. Then he walked to Sam's half-open door and tapped softly on it. "May I?"

"What a coincidence," Sam said. "I was just thinking that in all these years you've never met Mildred and the boys. Shimshon is coming next Saturday for Yom Kippur. Why don't you come too?"

"It's better I spend Yom Kippur alone."

"No one will ever accuse you of breaking a perfect record. Maybe next year." Sam shut the door and told Hyman to take a seat by the couch.

"Please. Would you sit at your desk and let me sit in the chair opposite you?"

"So formal?"

"I need to talk to you about a personal business matter."

"Oh. A personal business matter? Well, that's different. Why not have a coffee, tea or maybe a schnapps?" Sam said. "That's my standard business practice."

Hyman shook his head no. Only when Sam had settled comfortably into his desk chair did Hyman sit down. "I have one small question. Do you still keep money for me?"

"Of course." Sam leaned back in his chair. "Early in 1947, I started investing in equities. Half your money has always gone into one safe blue chip. AT&T. You've been quite a gambler with the other half, Mr. Schwartz. IBM. Last time my broker reviewed your portfolio, you were worth over one hundred thousand dollars."

"What?" Hyman said.

"That means you can afford new glasses."

Hyman pushed up his glasses and did a quick multiplication. The wages Sam paid allowed all the other men to support a house and family. So Hyman knew that he had to make more than the $2,600 a year he took from Sam. But $100,000 was a fortune.

"You've been lucky, Mr. Schwartz. Your money went into two of the Big Board's stellar performers. If neither of your stocks increases in value, which is highly unlikely, and if you stopped working today, you could live on that money here in the U.S.A. until the next century. Overseas you'd last forever. However you figure, you could support yourself for a long time. Maybe you'd consider a trip abroad. Someone I know would be thrilled if you traveled to Israel. Equities are liquid, you know. Do you want me to sell part of your portfolio?"

"Please. I'm not asking you to do anything." Hyman got out of the chair and walked slowly to the door, shaking his head in disbelief. "So much money."

"Wait a minute, Mr. Schwartz. I've noticed the terrible itch you have. Can I recommend a dermatologist?"

"I'm fine, Mr. Teitlebaum." Hyman shook his head. The one who needs help is God. "A hundred thousand dollars."

"More than one hundred thousand. Is that what you want to see me about?"

"I was just checking, Mr. Teitlebaum. Just checking."

Chapter Twenty-seven

YOM KIPPUR DAY, Saturday, September 15, 1956, was balmy. A cool breeze filled the air with vitality. Shimshon, Sam and the two Teitlebaum boys ambled into the Young Israel of Flatbush, the local Orthodox synagogue, debating whether the Dodgers, who were locked in a tight pennant race with the Milwaukee Braves and Cincinnati Reds, would make it to the Series and face Stengel's powerhouse Yankees. They meandered down the synagogue's center aisle, shaking hands and saying hello to friends as they headed toward their usual bench. The volume of conversation in the half-filled synagogue was rising to its traditional loud hum.

An annoyed congregant named Karpinski said, "Shh. Shh. The cantor's already been praying for twenty minutes. You're at Yom Kippur's Shaharit service, not at Ebbets Field."

Twenty-six hundred years and two diasporas had scattered Jews around the world. With neither Pope nor Vatican to unify practices, communities as far from one another as Baghdad is from Belz evolved their own traditions. Customs in Berlin bore scant resemblance to those of Hellenic Alexandria. Although the Young Israel of Flatbush followed Jewish Halakic Law as scrupulously as the austere Temple Beth El that Hyman had been carried out of, its atmosphere was entirely different, informal not refined, Sholom Aleichem not Heine, Galician not Prussian.

Sam sat down at nine twenty-five. "A cantor for the High

Holy Days costs over a thousand dollars," he told Shimshon. "Ours is a yeshiva student who really needs the money. But if you want a real cantor, go hear Kutzevitsky at the Beth Shalom in Borough Park. When he's not cantoring, he's singing at the Met. Do you see Herman Handleman, the gray-haired man up front?"

Shimshon seemed lost in thought. "Oh, yeah," he finally said.

"Last Yom Kippur he paid two hundred fifty dollars just to hear Kutzevitsky sing Kol Nidre." Sam raised one eyebrow to emphasize the price. "And in my book, to have once actually heard Kutzevitsky in person is getting more than your money's worth. Not that two hundred fifty dollars means anything to a man as rich as Handelman."

Sam opened his siddur, davened—prayed, in Orthodox Jewish parlance—and shuckled, a way of swaying forward and back that observant Eastern European Jews do as they pray. But after a moment of prayer, Sam nudged Shimshon. "Why would Hyman suddenly be interested in money?"

"Huh?" Shimshon answered as if shaken out of deep concentration. "He counts money all day."

"The man never gave a damn about personal finances. Now he wants to know how much money he has."

Shimshon seemed to ignore what Sam was saying, as if he were searching for the right words. He squeezed Sam's bicep tenderly. "I've got to tell you even if today is Yom Kippur. I bought a ticket. I leave Sunday, October twenty-first, El Al Flight Number One to Tel Aviv." Shimshon looked right at Sam. "Please understand. It's time."

Sam shut his prayer book. "Have you considered how Hyman will react?"

"I'll tell him Monday. He still hasn't said he won't move."

"The man's going nuts, pulling off skin like he has another layer underneath. Damn." Sam found the right place in his siddur, and prayed. "Forgive us Lord for this past year's sins, for sins of omission and commission, for sins of deception, for days we strayed so far from Your tent that like

171

sheep lost in the Judaean Desert, we could not hear Your sweet voice calling us to Ein Gedi and Jericho." Sam's eyes were moist. "There's so much noise over there lately, Shimshon, between fedayeen and Nasser. Why not let things simmer down before you go?"

"I might as well wait for the Messiah. It's time, Sam. You know it. I know it. I'm sure Hyman knows it too."

Across the river in Manhattan, in his room at the Excelsior Hotel, Hyman went to get his envelope for the hundredth time that day. He recollected this time last year when his screams had reverberated in Beth El: "You killed them. You did it."

Sitting pensively, Hyman felt tears welling in his eyes. Where's Mama? Why do I have to leave Rava? But I want to sell wood at a profit. Losing Rachel hurt so much that I shut out friends and lovers. If I hadn't said hello to Shimshon, I'd still be dead. What made me hide my heart? A cut so deep and fast that I looked down and couldn't believe my guts were tumbling out? Maybe the only way finally to forget is to remember. Hyman reached a trembling hand to the back of the closet and took out the envelope once more. It was time, he knew. Time.

He stroked the envelope with hands that kneaded love with sadness and remembered so many years of loneliness. He lowered himself into his chair. Trembling fingers unlaced the envelope; tear-filled eyes watched the flap yawn open. It's time, his inner conviction soothed him. Time. Welcome home. As he slid the pictures out and laid the stack face-down on his lap, he thought of Rachel, David, Mama, Papa, uncles, aunts, cousins and a two-year-long cloud of ashes drifting past Buna. A life. A family. A culture. A thousand years of civilization. Two thousand years of dreaming. All gone.

Shivering and short of breath, he cried. But for the first time since he had unearthed this envelope in Warsaw, for the first time since the leaden *now* had imposed itself unremittingly, he turned over a photograph and looked at it without fleeing. Rachel. Is that you on the steps of our apartment house? Your soft face is smiling, your loving eyes reach out

172

and embrace me. That's our son you're cradling. Nineteen thirty-seven was good and sweet.

Hyman remembered asking her to pose on those steps. "But he'll catch a death of a cold," she had said.

"Not him. You're holding the strong son of Hyman Schwartz."

"I'd rather he was gentle like his father," she had replied and smiled as Hyman snapped the photograph. Steps. Those were the same steps he had curled up on when he discovered that they, along with the two smashed columns, were all that remained.

Hyman took a deep breath and closed his eyes as he turned over the next photograph. If they had listened to his parents' ultra-Orthodox traditions, Hyman would never have this photograph. But while Rachel's family was willing to make many concessions to the Schwartzes' religiosity, they were modern and insisted on hiring photographers so they could record the wonderful day. And they hired a contemporary band so whoever wished to could celebrate it with men and women dancing together.

Hyman opened his eyes. The picture was from their wedding celebration. White lace, food, Hebrew words written across the flower-covered canopy. The marriage ceremony was beginning. Whole families were watching. But Rachel had turned around and was smiling through her veil's lace. Come to me my love. Be mine forever. Light me up with suns and moons and stars and a heaven of glittering lights. Lie beside me and soothe a heart that breaks to see you.

Hyman dug his fingers into his forearm, hoping that pain would reunite him with Rachel. But he quickly withdrew his nails. Mortifying flesh never brings your lover home. That's what life is really like. And if Rachel were alive, she would dance every dance to celebrate being alive. Rachel would never waste her one life to punish God.

Hyman stopped. Two photographs were enough for a day, maybe enough for a lifetime. Rachel and David. Rachel and me. Once I had the whole world. Now I've got an old room and

Shimshon to send on his way. But it's time. Time to say good-bye to Rachel, time to do what a Papa has to do for his son.

Hyman propped up the two photographs on his night table, and put the envelope back on its shelf. He felt not last Yom Kippur's rage, but sorrow's crystal clarity. Resting his brow on his forearm, he leaned against the wall and cried. All I loved turned to ashes. Little men. Little wars. Little sins. Little habits. Papa taught me two ways to say good-bye. I'll wave good-bye to Shimshon when he leaves. But for a small Jewish man like me, no matter what I think and feel about the One up there, the only way I know to say good-bye to Rachel and David is Kaddish. My faith may be gone, but my habits remain. Not that Rachel and David need my Kaddish. Dead people couldn't care less. But I do.

"Yisgadal veyiskadash schmei rabba." Hyman recited the Kaddish's first words. Ashes swirling over Buna settled on the black earth and mingled with the Polish countryside. A man harnessed himself to a plow and struggled with unyielding soil. Our families turn to ashes, our dreams turn to dust. Hyman said Kaddish, the language of his sorrow, the melody his father had given to Hyman's tears when their first furrows were cut. "He who makes peace in His heavens shall make Peace on this Earth, upon us and upon all the nation of Israel and say ye, amen." Rage dissolved in tears. Wrap me, hold me. Swaddle my sorrow. Wash me with the Kaddish that finally says the end and amen. Hyman wept without screaming. Who killed my family makes no difference because no matter who did it, my family is dead and gone. And with each breath I take I will miss them forever. He looked at the numbers on his forearm and at the scratches and scars surrounding it. In one final act of self-absolution, he stroked his arm, apologizing to it for so many years of abuse.

God, Keeper of the books of Life and Death, keeps no straight columns. No auditor ever checks whether His debits and credits match. But if by some chance there is a God and He can't keep a straight column, let Him worry about it. I've got enough problems of my own.

Chapter Twenty-eight

WHEN HYMAN AWOKE Sunday morning, wind was shaking the window casements, rain was showering their panes. He immediately turned on the light and looked at the pictures on his bedside table. Rachel's smile reminded him of spring mornings he had awakened to in Warsaw, when he had seen yellow daffodils, scarlet hyacinths and lavender irises veined with gold blooming in the courtyard. He remembered the softness of her skin when he kissed her cheek and recalled her murmuring, half in sleep, "Hi, sweetheart." Holding her picture lovingly, his hands trembled. He brought it toward his lips and kissed her. Where are you now, darling? Can you see my tears? Stay. When I come in from the rain, I need you here to make my heart sweet again.

When Hyman entered the office on Monday morning and greeted Faye, he sounded almost tender. "I hope your fast was easy, Mrs. Sondheimer."

"My waistline could use more than one day's fast, Mr. Schwartz."

Hyman had not been tempted to look before; but now he was curious. When Faye stood to hand him the day's work, he took stock. What she considered fat was that shapeliness he had loved in Rachel. Hyman knew how hips like that yielded when hands ran over them, how they responded when dancing.

Stirred by Mrs. Sondheimer, Hyman imagined himself waltzing with her and felt no guilt. He felt alive again. All morning he looked forward to seeing Shimshon. If only Shimshon's father could be here to see what a wonderful man his son has become, Hyman thought. And when Shimshon appeared at noon, Hyman told him immediately how absolutely excellent his worksheets were and how proud Hyman was to be his teacher.

Yet despite the praise, Shimshon made stupid, nervous jokes. Hyman understood immediately. But it took Shimshon until twelve forty-five to finally blurt out, "October twenty-first is over a month away. That's when I go."

Hyman reflected on the lunches and conversations they had had.

"Join me," Shimshon said. "Israel would welcome you."

"You see through your hopes." Hyman smiled sadly. "But Israel's a country. A dream there is still just a dream. When you come down from the highest hill and survey the land, you'll see that Jews there deceive one another for the same stupid reasons everyone else does. How can a smart man like you think that something he's never seen is wonderful?"

"Everyone knows."

"If everyone knew, everyone would be there. If I go to Israel, the first week everybody will be nice. But then they'll say, 'You should teach the younger men accounting. Israel needs your help.' A few weeks later some planner will get the bright idea that I should teach math to schoolboys. 'Don't worry,' he'll say. 'Teaching in Yiddish is okay.' But after six months I won't be new in the neighborhood. First they'll inquire, then they'll suggest, you know, that I learn Hebrew. How could I say no? If I live there, I *should* speak the language. Then the local yenta will say, 'Listen here, Schwartz. Israel needs Jews. Get married and have children.' And from her perspective, she'll be right.

"You got a dream, go to it. Just don't think Israel is going to give to you. A new country has a million needs. Every two weeks it will expect you to feed it more."

Shimshon leaned towards Hyman. "Don't slam the door shut."

"If you want to keep a door open, it's open. Just don't expect me to walk through it any time soon. My life is here now." The bells at St. Anne's tolled one. "Let's not gab any longer. I'm glad we have until October twenty-first. And I'm sorry we have so little time left. Believe me. Even if I wanted to go, I'd be a millstone." Hyman turned away and entered a number into Victor. "Just like Mr. Teitlebaum."

"What does that mean?"

"A man on his own should be on his own," Hyman said, his fingers prancing over Victor's keys. "And tomorrow we'll talk about Mr. Teitlebaum."

Hyman worked with ease and finished at five. He headed uptown. The rain had stopped but a mist hovered in the still air. His thoughts turned inward: Before Shimshon, my days were simple. In the morning I got blank worksheets, and at night I brought back finished ones. Then I started eating with him and got forty-five special minutes a day, minutes when an orange tastes like marmalade and when seconds sparkle like diamonds. Could heaven feel fuller than watching him learn, is sunlight brighter than his smile at some new discovery? What will I do without that special forty-five minutes? Will I spend my time kissing Rachel's picture every morning, whispering to her at night? Would my heart have been broken anyway watching David leave? Does your own son become a bastard too, strut in after you've taught him all that you know and announce that now he's the boss and either you do things his way or everything's over?

Walking past Macy's, Hyman saw his reflection in a display window. Cocking his head sideways, he studied the shabby man staring back at him. That man did not look like the man Rachel had loved nor the father David had admired.

"No," Hyman said to himself. "You're not fair to say that Shimshon's giving orders. Not fair to him, not fair to yourself." He fingered his overcoat's patches. "He treats you like a normal father. He's doing what every normal son has to do. No, you're not being fair," Hyman said to the eyes, his eyes, staring back at him from behind his Scotch-taped glasses. "You deserve respect and good treatment. If not from other people, at least from yourself. You gave Shimshon an education no college could match."

Hyman left the window slowly. At home, he sat gazing at Rachel, his wife. When I look at your picture, Rachel, my hand reaches into the paper, my palm remembers how soft your body was. I would trade this life and any hope of eternity to hold you in my arms for even a second. I would climb mountains, grovel and beg, even declare the Almighty my God forever. But turning to stone only made me forget how sweet your skin tasted, how precious your body felt when it melted into mine and took me in with wetness and warmth. I made myself forget a lot. Accepting that the dead stay that way forever freed me. But now I have to learn to undo God's greatest trick, to turn ashes into life. Be with me if I stumble, hold me if I fall. Good night my love. Let me kiss your eyes and send you to sleep.

At the next day's lunch Shimshon found reason to worry. Rather than talking about Israel or numbers, Hyman seemed off somewhere. Shimshon mentioned that a ticket to Israel was expensive and explained that the distance was so great that the airplane had to refuel in Manchester. He discoursed on the 1948 War of Independence. Hyman seemed not to hear. "Oh," he said absentmindedly. When Shimshon described the green Galilee, and the turquoise water and purple desert mountains of Eilat, Hyman muttered "Hmm," nodded, and spun a pencil.

Hyman was off somewhere until St. Anne's announced twelve forty-five. He snapped alert for a moment, his eyes ablaze. "Believe me. For your own good, don't be partners with Mr. Teitlebaum. No businessman who prides himself on how good a boss he is will let you run a firm your own way."

"Working with Sam beats working for somebody else."

"Rushing always was your weakness." Hyman leaned fiercely toward Shimshon. "Just move slowly! For once, be more like me! Keep your options open."

Chapter Twenty-nine

IN THE LAST WEEKS of September and into early October, Hyman assaulted Shimshon with stinging questions. "How will you feel when Sam comes to visit and, without even knowing the business day to day, begins making suggestions about what you ought to do? And how will you feel telexing Sam, your big foreign investor, that you've made some bad business decision that cut deeply into profits? How will you feel when Sam wants to come over and review the firm's ledgers? Just to be sure, you know? Or come for a long visit so he can immerse himself in the firm's daily workings? And will you still feel you're your own boss when you have to listen to Sam intimate that he thinks certain expenditures are frivolous?"

Shimshon found Hyman's logic flawed and his analogy cruel. "Think how well he got along with his last partner," Hyman would argue. But Hyman's insistence reverberated with Shimshon's own misgivings. When he was honest with himself, he had to admit that this partnership would feel like working half-time for an absentee landlord.

On October ninth, sun and warm air blessed the city. The Central Park reservoir reverberated with the cackle of geese resting on their trip south. Thankful for a reprieve, people carrying briefcases rushed to work without overcoats. They talked continually about the incredible perfect game Don

Larsen had pitched for the Yankees the prior day to put his team one up on the Dodgers in the Series. Today, the Yanks could end it all.

Hyman walked among the people, anticipating the day with relish. He was going to be the father he had always wished to become. The riot of colors on women's clothes pleased him: emerald jackets, floral dresses, and white silk blouses. The aromas at the delicatessen filled him with joy. Armed with the conviction that what he would ask Sam first thing this morning was thoroughly in tune with nature's own desires, Hyman bounded into the office, spoke to Sam, and went to his cubicle. He galloped Victor faster than ever before.

By eleven, when Sam gave him the figure he had asked for, Hyman had already finished the morning's work. He raced through half the afternoon's worksheets. He was so happy that at noon it took Shimshon's knocking hard on the glass to jostle him out of his reverie. "Come in. Make yourself comfortable."

Hyman had been so inconsistent for weeks, absentminded, lost in a cloud, challenging and belligerent about Sam, that Shimshon had worried he would end up in a lunatic asylum.

"Shimshon. Now that only ten workdays are left, do you smell how bad a partnership with Mr. Teitlebaum would be?"

"Not half as bad as working for strangers."

"Once in your life you go out on your own. Go like a free man. I don't want to hurt the boss. But to focus on what's best for you, I had to point out what's worst about him."

"The equation doesn't change. I'm happier being Sam's partner than a stranger's employee."

"We agree that needing capital makes you vulnerable. So first thing this morning I asked Mr. Teitlebaum to sell half of my stock." Shimshon was silent. "That's right. I have lots of money to bring to your firm. The boss didn't like my selling with no plan and said, like he always does, 'Won't you consider a smart investment I'm working on? I need your signature for anything but equities.' He even thought I wanted money to start my own firm. He said he'd be thrilled if I was independent. I figured it was better if I didn't let him in on our plan right away, so I said 'I knew you valued a man's independence. I'm glad you understand.' Actually, he looked confused but I didn't tell him the money was for you." Hyman smiled. "He isn't your only source of capital."

In a flash Shimshon concluded that Hyman meant to become his partner. He must be out of his shell, Shimshon thought, and he won't crawl back. He's not picking at his skin. And he's healed in more important ways. He's going to build a new life. Shimshon broke into a wide smile and hugged Hyman. "You're doing it! I can't believe you're coming!" Then he felt Hyman's body stiffen.

Hyman spoke softly. "If I was moving, I would have told you long ago. You don't need the partner problems with me that I warned you against having with Mr. Teitlebaum."

"If you put in money, you're a partner." Shimshon slumped back in his seat.

"No. When a good father gives a son a gift, he doesn't ask for partnership in return."

"I can't take your life savings and just walk away."

"Why not? You've got no father. I've got no son. I've got no use for this fifty thousand dollars or for the other fifty after it."

Shimshon put his elbows on the desk. "Please come along."

"You're the right age to go to Israel. I'm not!" Hyman stopped talking for a moment and rubbed his temples. "What's good for you isn't necessarily good for me. Whatever I say makes you feel bad because you want to believe I'm somebody I'm not. I want you to have children and to love them like I loved mine. Enjoy. Spend. Buy a house, car and clothes. Listen to music, look at art, read books and smell the flowers. Learn more. Study harder. But live. That's what a man is meant to do." Hyman touched Shimshon's hand tenderly and deliberately. "A man gets only one life. Let me worry about mine. Grab yours and make the most of it."

Shimshon sat silently beside the desk.

"Go back to work. My money's for you." Shimshon raised a finger in protest, but Hyman waved it off. "We have so little time. Let's enjoy it rather than arguing for two weeks. Tell me about your plans. But don't try to change me. I'm too old."

Without saying a word, Shimshon cleared the paper, orange peels and apple cores off Hyman's desk, shoved them into his Gristede's bag, and carried them back to his cubicle.

The moment Shimshon left, Hyman went to Sam's office.

"Come right in, Mr. Schwartz," Sam said and listened to Hyman's story without interrupting.

"When a man goes out on his own, he doesn't want a boss or partners," Hyman said as he finished. "I'm glad you understand a man wanting to be independent."

Sam slapped his hands on his knees and stood up. His eyes remained fixed on Hyman. "I understand a man who wants to be his own boss a lot better than I understand a man who doesn't." Sam's voice was tense. "What I can't figure out is what I ever did to make you conclude I was a first-rate son of a bitch you had to deceive this morning."

"What do you mean? You know I really respect you, Mr. Teitlebaum."

"You have a damned peculiar way of showing it." Sam pointed to his plaque. "Because of those words I feel like a bastard being angry with you. But I am. Without even talking over investments, you decided I was a money-grubber from the Lower East Side out to make a quick buck off a sucker kid."

"I never even thought such a thing. But Shimshon is a son to me. I'll never get another chance to make him independent."

"Hyman Schwartz. Kindest man in the world. Only you realized that Shimshon had to be protected from becoming unnecessarily dependent." Sam sat back down. "You've buried yourself in that cubicle for so damned long, you can't see beyond the Scotch tape holding your glasses together."

Hyman was perplexed. "I'm giving him money no strings attached. That's the selfish part. I'm giving him money because it's right for me."

"Do you really think you're the first person to figure that out?"

"I'd risk everything for him. Don't you see how important he is to me?" Confused, Hyman walked to the bookcase and moved his eyes from one gilt title to the next: *Don Quixote, A Farewell to Arms, A Room of One's Own.* "You've got so many fine things."

"So I'm too rich to care if you call me a bastard?"

"I'm begging you. Don't punish me by hurting Shimshon."

Sam was livid. "Get the hell out of here!"

"What did I do wrong?" Hyman had never seen Sam this angry. "You said the money wasn't important."

"But being called a sadist is. Don't you tell me that I'd hurt Shimshon. For over ten years I've adjusted to your *mishegas.* No more. This may come as a shock to you, but people other than you think that that fat-mouthed, red-headed prick is someone special. You don't want to know it. When I try to arrange things for him you barge in here like some new world Jesus Christ! Well, I'm angry at you."

"Please, I didn't mean to hurt you. I'm giving you the rest of my money. You don't lose a thing."

Sam turned blood-red.

Hyman was resigned. "If you fire me, I would understand."

"You understand *garnicht,* diddly squat, *nada.*" Sam stood up. "Go back to work. I'm not asking you to quit and if I want to fire you, I'll let you know."

"Please, Mr.—"

Sam interrupted. "When we have something to talk about I'll call you. Until then"—Sam held open his office door—"good day, Mr. Schwartz!"

Hyman trudged down the linoleum feeling dreadful but

proud. A time has to come when a man stands up for his son. The boss says money doesn't matter, but money is all that matters to a businessman. If it didn't, would he be so mad? That afternoon, whenever Hyman lost himself in Victor's rhythm, he soon faltered because he remembered Sam throwing him out with a frosty "Good day, Mr. Schwartz." You're not being fair, Mr. Teitlebaum. You're the one who told me to teach him. You're the one who sent him back until I said yes. Why do you want to keep him in your debt now?

Hyman tried to check invoices, but his eyes went out of focus. And in the blur, he reviewed their conversation, hoping to comprehend why Sam had misunderstood. Is there any chance he was angry not about the money I cost him but about something else? Maybe he wanted me to listen to his investment suggestion. He's taken good care of my money, so maybe I should have heard him out. But my idea was excellent. He's got no reason to be *that* mad.

What if Mr. Teitlebaum told the truth? But if he really was concerned about Shimshon's future, wouldn't he have smiled, said, 'Now I understand,' and shaken my hand for the good I'm doing? Truth is he must really dislike Shimshon. That was some vulgar name he calls him—that 'fat-mouthed redheaded prick'? Hyman reflected for a moment. But doesn't Mr. Teitlebaum always call his friends names like that?

A series of connections began to crystallize in Hyman's mind. That's your real reason for keeping your plan secret, isn't it? You don't want Shimshon to have another friend. Hyman rejected the idea, but it returned like a raven roosting on a mental ledge. The boss loves Shimshon too. So do lots of other people. By not telling the boss in advance, you said he wasn't Shimshon's friend. Hyman's mind began to race. I did act like a bastard. That's not the worst of it. If I had shared my idea, he probably would have helped me make even better plans. He never tried to cripple anyone.

Mr. Teitlebaum knows that what I'm doing is right. That's

not why he's mad. But I never imagined that an *alte cocker* like me could hurt a boss's feelings.

As his thoughts turned, Hyman wanted to burst into Sam's office and fall to his knees to apologize. But Sam had told him to stay away. The horrors God had inflicted were beyond comprehension. But today's sadness was over what he, one ordinary man, had done, not to gorillas and chimps, not to erect animals who wandered cityscapes, but to another flesh-and-blood human. And he was not the only one. For the first time since seeing placards waving at the *Leviathan*'s wharf, Hyman realized that the people holding those signs also had suffered and hurt. "Maybe you've seen my Shoshanah?"

Never before had he realized that all the firm's employees were also people. While he had suffered beyond what any human being could endure, all other humans were also wounded in their own ways. They also suffered, hurt and cried.

Hyman tried to forget and to finish work. But he broke a pencil point, put wrong figures into Victor and had to recalculate several times. Even then his computations did not match. Why didn't you see that the boss was Shimshon's friend? Did you think that he invited Shimshon home so many times for no reason? Or did you resent Mr. Teitlebaum because he has a home and you have none?

A soft knocking on the doorjamb broke the spell. "Mr. Schwartz?" Faye said. "Would you like a cup of coffee?"

Hyman looked at her soothing face. A coffee. A doughnut. A lunch. Lots of people other than Shimshon invite me. After my blackest hour Mr. Rossberg, an almost total stranger, invited me home. But I couldn't go. I would have spent all night staring at his son. How many times has Mr. Teitlebaum invited me? How many times has Mrs. Sondheimer brought me cake? When Hyman saw the invitations he had refused lined up, he shuddered. The rejections he had delivered and the pain he had caused looked like a row of tombstones.

"Mrs. Sondheimer. You just did more than you can imagine."

"I know how much it hurts you to watch Shimshon leave."

"But I'm happy that he's going."

"You're happy he'll be on his own, and you're sad that you won't have him here anymore. We'll all miss him. He's going so far away I feel like a relative is dying. You know, my Morris had cancer in all his bones. He cried all night for a year and begged for the pain to end. So when it finally stopped, part of me welcomed it. But even after two years, I still think about Morris and miss him all the time." Faye stepped into Hyman's cubicle. "I know that you and Sam had a fight. Shimshon heard about it, too. If you ever want to talk about it, just ask. But stay away from Sam. In a few days he'll forget why he's mad."

"But he has a good reason."

"Good reasons, bad reasons. Sam can't be bothered holding a grudge. It takes too much out of him." As Faye was leaving, an important observation stopped her. "You're a fine man yourself. If you made Sam angry, I'm sure you did it for the best of reasons. If they turned out to be wrong, what's the tragedy? We all make mistakes." Faye nodded. "It's true Mr. Schwartz. I wish I could take back some angry things I said to Morris in the last months or hold him tight and kiss him like he deserved for all the good years he gave me. But I can't go back and do it again. So you made a mistake. It couldn't be such a terrible one.

"And there's something else you should know, Mr. Schwartz. Don't you ever think that Shimshon is the only person who likes you. You're a fine man. A real gentleman. And don't you forget it."

Chapter Thirty

THE NEXT TWO DAYS were painful ones for Brooklyn. On October tenth, the Dodgers lost the World Series in the seventh game. Brooklynites and Teitlebaum & Sharfenstein went into mourning. That did not help Shimshon's cause. Every time he met with Sam in the next few days he begged the boss to relent. Hyman might be gauche, but he was not malicious. Of all people, Sam ought to realize that Hyman was just a man who had suffered too much. He asked Sam to consider how guilty he eventually would feel for what he was doing to a broken little man.

"If the man's so old and broken, let him mind his own business. My big mistake is that for ten years I've treated him like he was dead. You saw my error and approached him differently. I may not be a prince, but I try damned hard," Sam said, opening and closing the silver cigarette box. "In all of my dealings with Hyman Schwartz I was less than one hundred percent honest only once. Ever since, he's wrecked a perfect set of clothes to rub my nose in that."

"Listen to yourself! Do you think he dresses like a derelict to get even with you?"

"Not entirely." Sam drummed his fingertips on the chair arm, which seemed to calm him down. "Only in large part. From now on I don't care if he wraps himself in shit. But I'm finished giving him special treatment."

"What special treatment? You yourself said that Hyman's work is the best in the firm."

"Damn him!" Sam paced, stopping and pulling the Tabriz with his heel to straighten a kink in it. "He makes me sound like Sharp."

But for the next few days Sam obstinately refused to speak to Hyman. Four days before Shimshon's departure, at ten A.M., Sam told Faye to bring Hyman to the office.

"Be nice," she said.

"Just get him!" Sam replied.

Hyman knew that Sam had decided to fire him. He walked down the corridor staring stonily ahead.

"Do you feel all right, Mr. Schwartz?" Faye said.

"I'm fine, Mrs. Sondheimer. Fine," he said, accepting as just his appointment with the executioner. Bravely, he held his head high as he walked past secretaries, who stopped typing and whispered to one another as if viewing the doomed on his way to the guillotine. He walked into Sam's office and stood in front of the desk silently watching Sam review a long document with the standard light blue legal cover. Hyman knew what it was: the verdict, guilty as charged. The sentence: chop off his head. Sam signed the document and closed it.

"Ever since we spoke, I've been trying to arrive at a fair and proper decision." Sam's voice was formal. "You are the highest-paid accountant here. You earned that distinction with almost eleven years of uninterrupted excellence."

Hyman nodded gratefully, anticipating the *but*.

"But your actions speak loud and clear." Holding the paper he had signed in his hand, Sam walked around his desk and stood directly in front of Hyman. "Your recent actions are unfortunate. But neither of us can change the past. You put me in a very awkward position. If you owe me allegiance because I've been decent to you, it would mean that I spent over a decade helping immigrants just to earn their homage. While I like being appreciated, I've helped immigrants because I believe that helping people, not cheating, robbing or killing them, is what makes me a good human being and a good Jew, no matter what you think, Mr. Schwartz."

Hyman wanted to tell the boss how sorry he was, but before he got the first syllable out, Sam held up his hand for silence. "Although you insulted me, I have years of actions to show me the kind of man you are. For eleven years, no matter what time of day or night, weekday or weekend, if I had a hard account or a problem that needed a solution, you never said, 'I already put in my forty hours.' You just did it. You've earned your place here." Sam put his hands on Hyman's shoulders. "I guess we'll manage our way through a lot more years."

Hyman wanted to race out the door so Sam wouldn't see his tears. But until the boss dismissed him, Hyman could not leave. He turned away and dried his eyes.

"Come over here." Sam waited until Hyman had turned around. "This document empowers Shimshon to use your money. You'll have to sign it to release the check to him." Sam held out a pen. Hyman signed and smiled through tear-filled eyes. "I've drawn up a second document that empowers Shimshon's firm to handle the Israel end of my business." Sam sat down at his desk and pressed his hands together. "Just for the record, I won't be taking a percentage."

"I know I was wrong. I should have trusted you."

"But what you haven't realized is that the investment I had in mind for you was your putting up the money for Shimshon's firm."

"Oy, yoy, yoy!" Hyman slumped in the chair and looked at Sam. "I know I was wrong. And I know how much you'll miss Shimshon. I promise you that in the coming years I'll make up a little of the hurt."

"Please don't do me any more favors, Mr. Schwartz. Do yourself some. You may need your money some day."

"I do need five hundred dollars, Mr. Teitlebaum. There's a going-away present I want to buy Shimshon. I shouldn't ask you for any more favors on short notice. But please do me this one."

"It's your money. Spend it however you'd like." Sam swiveled his desk chair around. "You confuse me, Mr. Schwartz." Sam watched a flock of swallows swoop down from the sky like black raindrops, and flutter to rest on Broadway ledges. He put both his forearms on the windowsill, leaned forward, and rested his forehead on the windowpane. Without turning away from the swallows, he spoke again. "You just confuse me."

Chapter Thirty-one

AT THEIR NEXT-TO-LAST LUNCH, Shimshon voiced his concern. "I'm very worried about you. Why don't you take Faye out for coffee? She likes you a lot. Teach someone else. God damn it, do something for yourself. Letters aren't the same as lunch every day. What's going to happen when I leave?"

"I don't imagine I'll ever be the same." Hyman furrowed his brow as if, in deep contemplation, he were coming to terms with that fact. "No, I don't imagine I'll ever be the same."

Shimshon stood up and paced in and out of Hyman's cubicle. He turned the chair around, straddled the seat and folded his arms on the metal back. "At least move to a good neighborhood."

"Last year you started as a bastard who called a stranger family," Hyman said. "You were a boy then; now you're a man. Who ever would have imagined then that one year later you'd worry whether an old man moved to Flatbush, or that I'd agree that you're family?"

Shimshon smiled.

"Whenever the churchbells toll noon, I'll think 'Where's Shimshon now? Who is he eating lunch with?' Even though I'll know better, I'll look down the corridor half-expecting to see you coming this way holding your Gristede's bag." Hyman placed his hand on Shimshon's and looked straight into his eyes. "You've got a whole life ahead of you. Nothing gave me more pleasure than helping you live yours as a free man."

"You're beginning to sound like Sam." Shimshon pursed his lips and affected an authoritative voice. " 'Nothing in my life gave me more pleasure than helping immigrants.' "

"Mr. Teitlebaum's a smart man and must be a good father."

"So why don't you visit his family?"

"Stop pushing."

"You've done so much for me and nothing for yourself."

"You've done more for me than you want to imagine. But I still am handing you one small obligation. By taking my lessons and money, you are obligated to treat people well who are younger than you. Teach your son. Treat him nice." Hyman lifted his right hand and pressed his thumb and forefinger together. "Pffft," he said. "I think you can manage that burden."

"How could I ever do otherwise?"

"Good." Hyman smiled. "Then we both learned something. Time for you to go."

Shimshon started to ask a question, but Hyman insisted that they get back to work. Shimshon left, and went to Sam's office. "What's going to happen to Hyman after tomorrow?"

"Do you mean will he go crazy?" Sam said.

"Of course. Isn't there anything I can do to help him?"

"You can pack. Hyman's no infant. He'll do what he has to. He's changed more than I imagined possible. Little changes are what you get from men his and my age."

Shimshon paced Sam's carpet like an expectant father. "I can't sit still lately."

"You're doing great. Rossberg liked you. So did Finkelstein, Gold and Hymowitz. That's five accounts you've met and you've seduced every one. Pretty good for a loudmouth."

Shimshon smiled, and walked over to the windows to watch cabs speeding down Broadway; furriers, importers, wholesalers and retailers jostled one another on New York's streets. "Those accounts trust you, not me."

"Do you expect real businessmen whose families have dealt in precious stones for generations to take pretty-boy looks and nice words at face value? Those men are smart, experienced and successful. They take time before making judgments. But when they see that you also do quality work and are dependable, they'll trust you too."

"Do you ever regret we're not partners?"

"I have one firm to worry about. I'd just as soon let you and Hyman worry about the second."

"Can't I do something to help him? I still can't forget what you said! This is the same Hyman Schwartz who had to be carried out of synagogue."

"Something about Hyman has changed. Since I got mad at him, he walks around like a frightened puppy. He says hello to everyone, even seems worried that he might hurt someone's feelings. I don't know what he's up to, but something about Hyman has changed."

Chapter Thirty-two

ON THURSDAY AFTERNOON, Sam asked Hyman whether he wouldn't make an exception to his eleven-year-old habit and come to the conference room Friday afternoon for Shimshon's going-away party. To make the invitation more appetizing, Sam detailed the smorgasbord: bagels, lox, soft sable fish, Danish pastries, honeycake and two large urns of coffee in addition to a fully stocked bar. "So please come."

Even though Hyman was trying not to hurt anyone's feelings, he refused to commit himself and went back to work.

On Friday, a morning chill had replaced Indian summer. From eight o'clock on, accountants and secretaries shuttled in and out of Shimshon's cubicle. "So how's pretty boy doing?" "Take along Dramamine and Kaopectate!"

Sam worried because no one saw Hyman all morning. When he checked, Faye told him that Hyman had come to work at eight hunched over, with his hat pulled far down on his head. He had looked peculiar, even to her. But when she asked how he was, he had said, "Fine, just fine" and left.

At nine thirty Sam headed to Hyman's cubicle. From down the corridor he saw Hyman's overcoat slung over the doorjamb's crossbar and spread apart like a Do Not Enter sign. Sam returned to his office.

That afternoon, Shimshon met with Sam and told him that

Hyman had been so peculiar at lunch that he figured Hyman was going stark raving mad. Throughout lunch Hyman hardly spoke a word. He even refused to say good-bye, insisting life would give them other opportunities. For the first time since they had met, Hyman showed Shimshon a picture of his wife and son. "They were good to me," he had said. But most worrisome was that Hyman had sat hunched over frozen in his chair wearing his hat and overcoat. "It's cold again," he had said. "Winter's just around the corner."

Sam knew he would soon be calling some Park Avenue Sigmund Freud to help Scotch-tape Hyman's mind together. He went to Hyman's cubicle and found him hunched over Victor, which he had placed on the desk in front of him. As Shimshon had warned, Hyman was wearing his hat and overcoat.

"Aren't the radiators putting out enough heat?" Sam said.

Hyman kept working, and at first did not acknowledge Sam. Without turning around, he finally answered. "I'm busy. We'll talk some other time."

"When?"

"Some other time," he said and continued working.

At three thirty, accountants left their cubicles and secretaries pushed away from their desks. Everyone streamed to the conference room. Just inside the entrance, Shimshon stood shaking hands and hugging well-wishers. Jack Rossberg came, as did Finkelstein, Gold, Hymowitz and other accounts Sam had lined up for Shimshon. Men gobbled honey-brown bagels and toasted with Jack Daniel's and Chivas Regal. Salutations flowed as exuberantly as the liquor. "*L'Chaim*. To your health." "God bless you, Sam, for a spread like this." "Here's to Shimshon."

By three forty Hyman had not come.

Shimshon was slapped on the back and tapped on the shoulder. Himmelstein told him, "Come back this time next year. We'll have another party when we teach those Yankees how baseball is really played." Co-workers shook his hand; secretaries kissed him. Good luck. God. Isn't this lox delicious? "Hey, Sam?" Abromowitz saluted. "Where did the commander in chief buy sable this tender?"

Sam stood on a chair and raised a glass of Chivas. "To Shimshon." He chugged. Everyone followed and cheered. "*Mazel tov.*" "Good luck." "Here's to you. *L'Chaim.*" An adorable young secretary grabbed both of his arms. "God, are you going to make some pretty girl happy." She kissed him and quickly hurried away.

When Hyman had not come to the conference room by three forty-five, Sam pulled Shimshon away from Abromowitz. "Do you think I should look in on him?"

"Send Faye. She knows how to handle Hyman."

Faye was glad to go. But no sooner had she stepped out of the room—long before she could have reached the end of the secretaries' section—than Sam, Shimshon and everyone else in the conference room heard her exclaim in a loud, almost alarmed voice, "Mr. Schwartz!"

A few seconds later she returned, stunned. Hyman was right behind her. Walking in shyly, he had a fresh haircut. He had taken off his tattered overcoat. His suit was still brown, his shirt white, his tie paisley and his shoes wing-tips. But they and his glasses were brand-new.

The room hushed as secretaries and accountants who over the years had become accustomed to Hyman's tatters riveted their eyes on the small man, almost handsome in his new suit. Shimshon rushed up to him. "You're wonderful."

"I told you not to worry." Hyman was embarrassed to have drawn so much attention to himself. But he had wanted to surprise Sam. "Please. Please," he said. "Please eat. Please let's celebrate Shimshon's future." Knots of people unwound, talking in murmurs that rose and increased in warmth and levity until the room filled with so many *L'Chaims*, *Mazel tovs* and good lucks, that to relieve the tension Sam threw open a window. "Smell that delicious air." He came back and stood beside Hyman smiling. "Thanks."

"And now do you really forgive me?"

"I forgave you before."

"No. Before you were still hurt. You've been a very good boss, Mr. Teitlebaum. I wanted you really to understand."

Shimshon grabbed Hyman and shook him. "You crazy bastard!"

Tears filled Hyman's eyes. "I'll miss you." Hyman held both Shimshon's arms, looked him in the eyes, and for the first time in their year together, hugged him tightly. "I'll miss you every day. Make a good life for yourself."

So many people wanted to say good-bye that Shimshon had just a moment to smile with enormous gratitude at the man who had treated him like a son. Then Karnovsky turned Shimshon around, said, "Hey Jimmy Dean," and showered him with "good luck"s. Hyman excused his way through the crowd and meekly made his way to the table's end. "Mrs. Sondheimer?"

Faye smiled. "What a nice surprise."

"I know I've waited a long time. Let me finally thank you for caring. And if it's not asking too much, maybe soon I can take you for coffee."

"I'd like that," Faye replied.

Hyman walked over to the bar and poured two glasses of Chivas. In Rava they knew vodka and slivovitz. But Scotch? He carried the glasses over to Sam and handed him one. "To our mutual good friend." Hyman lifted his glass in a toast. "And to your continued good health, Mr. Teitlebaum. *L'Chaim.*"

And with that toast to life, Hyman ended so many years of loving solely the dead. He never forgave God; nothing could apologize for what He had taken. But in saying a secular Kaddish, good-bye to Shimshon and thank you to Sam, Hyman Schwartz reentered the world of vulnerable, suffering humans.

His worries about Shimshon had not ended. A few days after Shimshon flew off from Idlewild Airport, the Suez war broke out. Unconfirmed news reported Tel Aviv and Jerusalem bombed flat. "Is he okay?" the office buzzed. Who would have imagined? Is God going to kill my second son? Hyman worried. He started courting Faye and was grateful for her afternoon visits and soothing words. "He's a smart boy with a good education. He'll do fine."

On November 4, 1956, newspapers, radios, televisions and the bulbs circling the *Times* building carried the news. The Hungarian attempt to be free had ended. Russian troops had occupied Hungary. Hyman worried that it was a bad omen for Shimshon. Faye disagreed. The news only confirmed how smart Shimshon had been to leave Hungary when he had.

When Sam came to the office on November sixth, a cable was waiting for Hyman. He brought it to Hyman's cubicle.

Hyman was afraid to open it, frightened of the bad news everyone knew war brought. Accountants and secretaries waited outside his cubicle and whispered. "What is it?" "What does it say?" Sam motioned for them to hush; everyone knew Hyman's situation and waited quietly outside.

Rachel. David. Miss Greenbaum. Moscow can take forever. So many cables never come, Hyman thought. And just when I hope for none, this one arrives. With trembling fingers, Hyman unsealed the telegram. Breathing deeply, resigned to condolences, he read its words: ARRIVED SAFELY. JERUSALEM QUIET. LOVE TO SAM, FAYE, ABROMOWITZ AND THE GANG. AND LOVE TO YOU, MY DEAR, DEAR FRIEND. SHIMSON.

Hyman walked out of his cubicle slowly, and handed the cable to Abromowitz. "Let's share the winner's circle." He went back to his cubicle, listening to the chorus of shouts, cheers, hallelujahs and "Thank God"s outside his doorway.

The cable had arrived. The second son had arrived. Jerusalem doesn't take forever. And with that knowledge, Hyman smiled gratefully. He settled into his day's work exuberant. Shimshon is alive. Shimshon is well. He'll build a fine life for himself. God bless Shimshon.

Numbers raced through Hyman's fingers like ballet dancers. They went up on pointe every time Victor added, and plié'd when he subtracted. A *one* never changes. Shimshon's no cripple. He's safe and on his way. I let him go, no questions asked. What a boy! He's some man! Hyman was deeply pleased.

And Victor's narrow white paper racheted one notch higher.